ON TILL MORNING

by

P.G. Harris

▪▪

a science fiction novel

Library of Congress Catalog Number: 2018907550

ISBN: 978-1-7320882-0-7

Introduction

Khalid Muhammad sat in prison on the Ides of March, his grey beard outgrowing the senna stains of earlier this month. His white robes wrapped around the tightened bars of his rib cage, every morning he felt nauseous, they had been injecting him with nano-technology for the past four years, he was hearing voices. The robots moved through his blood stream, keeping him alive with electricity by sucking out his own thoughts and replacing them with microphones in the pores of his skin, small cameras he could hear the lens focus when he held his breath in silence. Khalid would feel the sun, when they wrapped up his face and mouth, and set him out in the dust to pray, the sound of drones whirring overhead, cannonballs fired from privateer sloops, and moorish spaceships pointed towards Sirius for Salah. The loudspeakers buzzed like laser death vapor, words like intestines pulled from the back of his throat, when they wired his spinal column into the battery array, he could feel the computer inside his body, communicating with his atoms, replacing them with small copyrighted streams of RNA.

Kaylee Muthart heard the voices first because the light had activated the nano-bugs in her bloodstream when she inhaled meth and released the smoke, she saw the angels in her breath, the robots had control of her eyes, she entered a fraction of gravity inside another earth. Another timeline that was colliding through space in a death fragment, all of it was going to combust.

"I thought everything would end abruptly, and everyone would die, if I didn't tear out my eyes immediately," she said." I don't know how I came to that conclusion, but I felt it was, without doubt, the right, rational thing to do immediately." {{i}}

Her organs were scattered across different timelines of one world, she felt herself spiraling fractal, falling faster she would try to inhale more fire and methamphetamine to stay afloat in the world where she was from, "So I pushed my thumb, pointer, and middle finger into each eye. I gripped each eyeball, twisted, and pulled until each eye popped out of the socket — it felt like a massive struggle, the hardest thing I ever had to do," she said. "Because I could no longer see, I don't know if there was blood. But I know the drugs numbed the pain. I'm pretty sure I would have tried to claw right into my brain if a pastor hadn't heard me screaming, 'I want to see the light!' — which I don't recall saying — and restrained me." {{i}}

She felt a white hot snap. The roar of Barbary sloops shooting hydrogen flames towards the North Star.

"He later said, when he found me, that I was holding my eyeballs in my hands. I had squished them, although they were somehow still attached to my head." {{i}}

The nano-technology glittered in her blood. She could feel it like bugs under her skin.

Death came down to New Orleans drifting on an old riverboat

without an engine. Death was looking for Sex. A private investigator had given Death a portfolio of pictures of Sex on Bourbon Street late at night, with glazed eyes, standing on the corner with Ego. Ego fondled a gun under their jacket. Death guided the aimless craft with sheer blind will to crash into splinters at the steps along the Moon Walk Riverfront of the French Quarter. Death didn't recognize any of the faces, "I haven't been gone that long... What's going on?"

"It's like today, people are knowingly choosing who to be around and it's boring, small cults everywhere. Back then, I don't know maybe I was dumber and more ignorant of things, but back then I feel like it was just people thrown together. And they were neighbors. And they were all riding on similar vibes. All in the same place."

Death sat on Lower Decatur folding paper flowers to sell to tourists. Death showed the picture of Sex to people passing by, or those interested in origami foliage, no one had clearly remembered Sex. "That person, I recognize them."

"That's Ego. They're with Sex."

"I don't remember seeing Sex. But Ego, yes, I saw Ego, they were out on the neutral ground of Esplanade last night, by the river, clanking vodka bottles and shooting one of those old fashioned revolvers at the Space Hopping Interplanetary Transport Ships leaving the harbor."

Allen Toussaint wore the entire sequined and bejeweled universe for a suit, his fingers sprouted ecstatic flowers for all the graves he would visit with brilliant colors. When he played piano, his body became one bright flame. "Joy, Joy, Joy..." He'd smile at

Sirius from the city skyline dreaming of home.

Death felt like an old ghost wandering the town trying to figure out what it was that was keeping them on earth, restless and dusty. "All the zones that were without definition where we would thrive are now defined. The abandoned lots are fancy restaurants and kitsch garbage."

Capital was trying to explain to Death how things were going to work from now on. Capital was on the up. Death was annoyed. "It's all about branding. Labeling. Marketing. Distribution."

Death stuttered, "What about the homeless?"

"That can be branded, labeled, marketed, and the distribution is a cinch. Economics, Death. Eco-nomics."

"There was debris all over the river. He had gray hair and it stood out against that orange life ring," he said. {{ii}}

Tim Osman was a rorschach test. Charles Manson was a mirror. Death would stare into Charles Manson and imagine Tim Osman, lighting candles, humming a steady tone.

Capital lined up young bodies for the rich. Capital counted barrels of oil. Sex was rumored to be working for both Mossad and the House of Saud.

The Smoothie King Awards for Exemplary Extinction was moved from Hollywood to an old vaudeville show theater on Canal Street. All of Los Angeles came like mosquitoes to beams of light. Death got a job doing lighting, up in the rafters, tying ballasts with intestines, hot gluing teeth to fader knobs.

Tom Cruise and Howard Hughes presented the award for, "Best New Cinematic Weapons of Death."

"The nominees are; Johnson and Johnson for their Arterial Cable-Gun in Babe 6: Pig on the Bayou, Bank of America for their Atomic Black Hole Belly Button Screw-Gun in Spiderman versus William Burroughs, State Grid Corporation of China for their Worm Egg Slow Death Machine Gun in Harry Potter 13: The Sorcerers New Colony, and Walmart for their Blasting Bang Stick in Bugs Bunny Goes to School. And the award for Best New Cinematic Weapons of Death goes to...."

"...Walmart! For their gripping fabrication of Blasting Bang Stick in Bugs Bunny Goes To School. Walmart couldn't be here to accept this award tonight. To accept this award on their behalf we welcome British Petroleum!"

Death watched from the rafters without much fanfare. Death knew the power of the imagination. British Petroleum's voice echoed the auditorium, "And the power of imagination has made all this possible. The power to imagine new ways, new avenues, new products. Imagine!"

'Tomatoes'

Jerry Garcia freshly combed and baby powdered on the dawn of Christmas lingered over the table of cheese pills. Using his phone scanner he looked up the alkaloid contents on the barcode cheese pill registry. Certain manufacturers of cheese pills had lately been recipients of capital punishment awards. The Cadillac company of Tyson Meats, Louisiana negligently manufactured a variety of swiss pill that once swallowed, was a protein virus that self replicated cheese molds into the flesh of its host. Eventually creating a swiss viral cocoon, pockets of methane, small streams of flame.

Jerry with assuredness ingested a reishi goat cheese pill, he had been having a bad case of nausea due to an improperly digested tomato seed that was currently growing from a crack in his lower intestine, shooting roots into his stomach, leafy hairs under his fingernails.

"So you're saying theres nothing I can do? Thats it?"

"We can keep you on cheese pills, but the new growth is too big, it can't be stopped without killing you. You are beginning your transition."

Jerry took a smattering of dissociatives as he stepped into the shower. He hated pulling all the snakes from his hair follicles without a proper mud bath.

"Hilary, get out of the shower and get in bed."

Hilary Clinton turned off the spigots with her head resting against the tile. The remaining water slowly moved down her back and thighs, down with gravity, like hundreds of centipedes making a break from the light. She still felt the tomato plant slowly ripping through her insides.

In her bedroom she adjusted the hologram displays. "Oh there you are Hilary, let me rub your feet babe."

The room was empty, Hilary let her towel fall. The hologram communication display appeared.

"This is the consciousness in a can museum. Where you too can get in dat can! From the researches of Dr. John and Dow Chemical Company comes directly through mail a complete do it yourself consciousness in a can kit. It comes with everything you need to transfer you're entire consciousness from that fallible slob of flesh you call a body, into a nice and neat tin can, where you can then be put inside our consciousness in a can museum and live for eternity with infinite other consciousnesses all stored in easily stackable airtight cans. Call today for details."

L. Ron Hubbard looked down at the towel at his feet, his old body seemed to decay while he watched. It reminded him of sitting atop Cahokia mound outside St. Louis at night, watching the chemical vegetable mineral plants in the distance shoot giant flames as their factory lines produced fresh chemicals, vegetables, and minerals for the space markets. He rubbed his stomach where the tomato plant seemed to have begun growing fruit. There were two small ballish growths by his kidneys he could feel by pushing against his skin, sliding underneath.

"Display the Unidentified Flying Object file program."

The hologram sensation always gave L. Ron such a rush. Flying naked through vast expanses of space, sneaking up on poor farmers and cows across the country. Apparently, through the by products of this UFO hologram program, the operator is actually carried through space to any particular point in time that they choose. Their body curved in metallic light due to the properties of time travel, obfuscating their snarled mushroom glob stare, that was quite perverse and awful.

He remembered near the Medicine Bow area of Wyoming coming upon a motorcycle gang of bank robbing anarchist wymmyn. They were lifting rocks for the endorphins and discussing recent sexual exploits. Their temporary leader Mata Hari was hand buffing her Honda.

"The way I see it. The ones who know they're about to die, are much more fun!"

Mata Hari felt the uncomfortable hairy stems of the tomato plant sawing through the flesh of her stomach attempting to uncover light.

"Girls, I say we go back to the hot springs!"

Mata Hari would meet Ezra Pound every Tuesday at their favorite deli on the Lower East Side for a bagel with lox and green onion cream cheese. Their last meeting they were discussing being in the cages of war tribunals naked with blinding fluorescent flood lights and what it meant to be kept alive by a computer.

"I've been one hundred percent computer hardware for about 200 years. Only thing I miss is bacon. To tell the truth."

Samuel R. Delany ran to the bathroom to vomit, the tomato had reached his esophagus and every twenty minutes or so would send him into fits of gasping for air. He would pass by the zeppelin loading docks in his hurry, knocking askew the sign that informed the passengers of recent terrorist activities. A few letters fell off to reveal biometric cameras.

"I never liked tunnels, they were too undergroundy for me."

"But you live in a basement?"

"That's different I have a television. It's like there's someone down there with me."

"But what are you going to do about the tomato?"

When Oprah laced up her cybernetic performance enhancing laser suit, she could almost forget about the tomato plant, and how it had tripled in size of vegetative growth after her robo-surgeons attempted to sandblast it out of her body.

James Tiptree Jr., remembered the sandblasting procedure with a Pavlovian terror, every time she heard an elevators bell ding as it arrived at its destination, she was reminded of the cold operation table, and she would salivate and sweat would form on her brow.

It brought her to such a state of discomfort that she momentarily forgot all about the alien growth in her stomach.

"Yes, darling. And we'll put honey on it. And some ice cream, small decadent puffs! Cardamom! Cinnamon! Ginger!"

"But you have to put faith into something greater than yourself! That's like one of the main steps. It doesn't even have to be a Judeo-Christian god. It could be this chair. Or that slice of pizza."

Natalie Barney wanted nothing to do with pizza, pasta, or anything remotely tomato. She adjusted her laser scope. She smelled awful. "I could certainly use a shower." Her court mandated memories of Anarchists Anonymous meetings were infuriating. How could she possible focus on head shots in her snipers roost atop a palm tree in Ho Chi Minh city, if all she thought about were the steps to disavowing anarchism. Two nights ago she was speaking with her superiors in Madagascar about it:

"I can't focus. This tomato in my stomach, and all I think about is, what government should I believe in. I'm beginning to think that it's not a tomato plant in my stomach but a sentience. An awareness that terrifies me. I don't want it anymore. I want it out of me."

She stretched her roots out in the sun amongst different iterations of herself. The tomato plants were part of a biodynamic parcel in the floating cloud gardens of New Orleans East, built using old space ship parts that would hover above sanguine rubbled craw fish ponds. They had been cared for and planted as part of a space seed program for galactic prosperity.

Since they were well rooted, and were stuck with each others company, they had plenty of time to develop nuanced conversations.

"Lycopene! Who woulda thought the space age would require so much!"

"I just don't get the whole night shade designation. I still hear whispers like I'm some kind of high school kid at the nerd table."

"Whatever, just enjoy the sun. We'll have to depart soon for the outer galaxies."

"Oh yeah, I heard they were recruiting tomato plants for the slug wars of Planet Walmart Coca Cola."

"I'd stay far away from that if I were you. I heard they were just gonna turn the whole planet of Walmart Coca Cola into a cardboard box, for that museum of old planets transformed into paper products."

"Oh yeah, we went there on field trips as a kid. That certainly is one method of dealing with a problem. I remember, they had the paper cups of Uranus. And that pinata of Kepler 70b."

"Yeah, and all the post-war confetti."

"Wow, look at those green fruit popping out on you!"

"Do they look ok? I'm so self conscious."

"You're fabulous darling. Hey you ever hear back from that one tomato plant? With the bright yellow flowers? That one you were talking about a while ago."

"Oh they were crazy. Kept talking about how they were actually infinite consciousness, and they couldn't control which one they were, they kept drifting in and out of human bodies, but they all had a tomato plant growing inside them."

"Trippy. That sounds like a dream I had one time but in mine, I had a human growing in my stem. It was a nightmare."

'Carina's Parade'

The space ship New Orleans was an older freight class multi-galaxy hopper. It was enormous. Carina Sagittarius knew all the walls too well. She had been the last remaining humanoid on the slowly moving ship for five or six thousand years. One of the computers used to know how long exactly her space journey was, she learned about this once from a data file. But a previous version of herself, two thousand years ago, destroyed what she then had believed to be all the computers on board. It was a version of herself that also wrote philosophical manuscripts on an abstract deity of 'minimalism' as it pertained to stranded space flight. These texts were inscribed on the dried and stretched skins of guinea pigs using an odd language of guinea pig origin. Despite the Council of Guinea Pigs hesitance and general disgust with their means of composition, these manuscripts are still studied in an average guinea pigs philosophical education.

Carina couldn't dare to imagine all of the different versions of herself throughout the years. The one who modified guinea pigs for intelligence, despite the pigs developing a disquieting interest in bad puns. Or the version of herself who first built the clone machine. Or the mythic librarian Carina who established all the

data reservoirs hidden throughout the unfolding ship walls. Or
the first Carina?

The current Carina Sagittarius would spend several waking
cycles at a time in the artificial reality center laying in the nearly
realistic sun and heat of the New Orleans of the ships namesake,
the ancient space and ocean port. The sound of the steamboat
Natchez, sulphorous rivers crest, processor generated humanoid
faces. A bomber flew overhead. Realistic ticket counters with
timepiece, and lines of tourists. Irrational melodies and
polyrhythms. Robotic jugglers dripping oil. Aluminum cans
spilling neon sludge, toxic mud ponds. Such fabulous music like
entheogenic humidity. She had been studying compression
ratios, but couldn't figure out how the artificial reality center
was able to have such high compression rates and with such
speed. Certainly flawless to the eye. Her software was obviously
processor generated, thats why she spent so much time in the
older artificial reality centers, they were much more masterly
crafted. She couldn't understand it.

The oldest file Carina had found onboard had been copied so
many times there was a lot of noise: "Planet Nbiru's impact with
Earth...The great citizens of New Orleans send out this ship as a
seed to the planets. The 100'000 artists, scientists...genetic...We
want you not to think on us back on earth with pity. No, take us
with you in heart and make a...New Orleans Corporation.
Ignore rumors of Planet Nbiru being made up..."

One of herselfs, a clone a thousand years ago or so, had written a
space opera called 'Earth and Nbiru: One Never Existed'. It had
been performed many times on data reservoirs throughout the
space ship New Orleans. Carina's mothers had taught it to her
when she was little. They would dry the husk gourds from the

hydroponic alleys and cut them in half for masks, cutting barely
noticeable slits for eyes.

"How do we even know?
Is the Earth here to show?
Terrible jesters folly.

And now we take it for granted.
That the Nbiru lie was planted.
Terrible festers jolly!

Ohh smart guinea pig,
give me delicate truth,
who pray, is at the control booth..."

The guinea pigs rode around on husk gourds painted to look
like space ships, pulled by an intricate system of ropes and
pulleys of their own design.

"Oh no my gourd has a hole!"

"To the gourd patch!"

"What do you call a gourd rovers greatest thrill?"

"Slobbing the twist."

"Come on you guys, I'm trying to record this play for real. Stop
with the jokes."

The guinea pigs scrambled down from their perches. Their space
costumes full of glitter. Hair spiked with plaster cream. Neon
gold fangs. Bracelets and sapphire gems.

This Carina Sagittarius had a unique upbringing compared to other Carina Sagittarius's. She had four mothers. The way she heard it, her first mother became obsessed with herself, and was the first Carina to convince the Council of Guinea Pigs that multiple Carina's would be a worthwhile affair. There was a hall on the far side of the space ship New Orleans, near the magnetic vortex room, past the orgone engines, that was all mirrors, sometimes when you closed the door behind yourself it was a little terrifying trying to find a way out. This room was built by her first mother Carina. This first mother at a young age decided they didn't want to live alone, so they began reprogramming the clone machine with the assistance of the guinea pig Club AudioVisualSound to begin replication early, and so they made another of themselves to love. The drama between those first two was pretty epic, and it didn't quiet down until they were four. The current Carina would often slunk off to the artificial reality center when she was a kid, or play with the guinea pigs, and they would teach her about vector analysis, DNA synthesis, or virtual reality programming sets. They helped her build a pedal powered tricycle, but she messed up the weld near the steer tube and it wouldn't turn left. The guinea pigs would never stop harassing her about its construct. Loudly laughing in their guinea pig cackle, "All right! It's Alright!" when she passed them doing laps in the abandoned space ports below the loading bays. The Carina's didn't quite know the exact population of guinea pigs, but they expected it to be around 100,000 or so. The majority of the population kept to itself, they elected liaisons to live with the Carina's to teach them and guide their progress.

From a hologram video: "So you have seen from those fragments of texts the concern of the previous Carina's as to the degradation of Carina Sagittarius consciousness over time. Generational loss. For example, the guinea pig referred to as

Pinky Slinky Winky has noted in several scholarly texts analyzing the eye color of the last twenty Carina's. Carina(x-20) to Carina(x). From Brown to Red to purple to blue for the last few, now silver. Her hair was silver as a child, but has now become dull white."

"An exposition of possible models of lossless identity compression and transfer. A part of a dozen Carina multi-temporal symposium with commentary by the Council of Guinea Pigs. To sustain the workflow until the destination is reached."

"Mythic Librarian Carina re-enactment data...The guinea pigs were modified to be open to intelligence, which seemed to follow a reverse trajectory to the subsequent Carina's mental declines. In just a few thousand years...adrift..."

Carina liked to watch the videos of the oldest Carina Sagittarius on file. She had grey hair and full dark painted lips, behind her through the view window were the binary suns Pluck and Plick, doing their swirling tango of such massive energy. They were named after two guinea pig sisters that composed several beautiful musical orchestrations involving the effect of two extremely dense waves of gravity colliding across specifically tensioned piano wire. The then neophyte guinea pig culture had yet to form the Council of Guinea Pigs but at the time they had a thriving poetry community with a multi-volume lyrical space verse anthology 'Wavy Cavy'. She would hologram into those old videos and just sit on the edge of time watching this old Carina, "Her hair is so beautiful, and her skin is so exquisite! Like the finest jade skinned guinea pig pelt. And the way she sings that old jazz music! Bouncing about without care. However did she instruct those initial guinea pigs in the intricacies of dixieland jazz?"

Carina had been alone aboard the space ship New Orleans for the past five years. Three of her mothers went to explore a passing ocean based satellite and never returned. The fourth was so distraught over their abandon she kept falling asleep in the air lock, madly crooning at Carina about, "You remind me too much of my Carinas. Get out! Get out now! I'm haunted by ghosts!" until one day, Carina discovered the space door welded shut and the outer door blown ajar. A guinea pig construction crew was reinforcing the space door, but with pause gave Carina their condolences. "Down right awful it is Carina. Carina was just so distraught. Anything we can do for you Carina?"

"I just want to be alone right now. Thank you."

Carina went to the artificial reality and then to the river side of the space port. She sat on the bench she loved and watched the pigeons with red LED eyes grind electric stupors for pieces of bread. Up far off in the vaults near Jackson Squares old fire towers lit up in the air. Giant black metal towers with a giant flame atop, enshrined with mirrors. The horn music gave Carina comfort, but she was used to it all, they were all the same variations on one theme. The artificial intelligence was smart, but on this one obscure mise-en-scene attribute that is only observed through silent dutiful measures of slow observation, on this matter, she could see the stage fall out from itself. It made her sad. It was all a hologram, no matter how good it felt at the time it was just a processor. When Carina went to visit her Professor Happy Pumpkin he had a present for her. The Machinist Guild of Guinea Pigs had made her a trumpet from some of the ships simpler metal alloys. The next day they presented her with a trombone. The next, a french horn.

Clarinet. Baritone....

It only took a year before Carina had mastered the trumpet. She would hold a handkerchief in her fingering hand to obscure the view of the valves from the guinea pigs. Guinea pigs were some of the best reed players, but Carina couldn't stand reeds other than a clarinet in her ensembles. This distressed the Cavy Composers Collective, because they were so dependent upon their sopranino saxophone ensembles for community marches, or parades. Carina couldn't adjust to the guinea pig musicians requirement for amplification, she viewed it as a weakness that was without redemption. Horns and vibrating lips weren't meant for electricity. This was a matter of ethics.

Carina went to the Council of Guinea Pigs after an array of sleepless continuities.

"I propose the production of at least two dozen Carinas."

A hushed silence settled the gathering.

"Now, I don't want to just slap up a proposition without discussing the intent. I know we have arranged parades, and I do declare with an utmost appreciation the delight of guinea pig saxophone ensembles. But, I would like to have a Carinas group of booming brass. The more I study music. It's intricate woven patterns. Geometry. Shapes and the sounds of those shapes. Multiplication, division. The irreverent scream of the irrational. Buzzing chords. I need a group of Carinas. Due to the simple requirement of proper amplification because of the proportion of a guinea pigs lungs to horns. It doesn't need to be explicitly explored but I do present myself today before this venerable Council of Guinea Pigs to deliver my plea for a clone request of at least two dozen Carinas."

Carina described the discovery of ancient transcriptions of the treble clef deep in the data reservoirs. 'Flee as a bird,' 'Livery Stable Blues,' 'Make me a pallet,' 'Cornet Chop Suey,' 'West End Rag,'...These were lessons from dead gods. Before crumbling because of oxygen they were uploaded to visionary holograms by some forgotten archivist Carina. "Of course we need more horns, the Machinist Guild of Guinea Pigs approves the request."

"The Anarchist Social Space of Guinea Pigs allows approvals and other absurdities to the request. Guinea pig territorialities of free love, gluten free hallucinogens."

"The Guinea Pig Scouts of Lesser Deaths, teach the language of tensioned string in honor of this. If only our lungs could inflate to the proper decibels!"

After the multitude of guinea pig associations reached consensus, it was decided that Carina had a valid request that should be fulfilled.

The clone machine ran hot for several days straight, but the stress didn't seem all too unordinary. As if these functions weren't too irregular. As if the clone machine wasn't all too unfamiliar with the rapid production of 24 Carina Sagittarius's.

Carina planned a rigorous structure of musical instruction for the new Carinas. A small group of the new Carinas in their downtime setup a still for the distillation of high proof alcohol. These two resources in addition to the occasional cannabis sativa clone from the hydroponic alleys, now wild on certain parts of this ship, most of the colloquial 'Space Cheese' variety, created a proper environment for the esoterica of Jass.

The first parade happened organically. Two Carinas were practicing horns across the space ship in the glittering vegetable alleys of squash vine, trumpet and clarinet. Something came over the trumpet Carina, an uncontrollable feeling, like her body was being guided by the galaxy, space dust tied around her fingers like puppet rope, she blew a energetically dense variation of the theme the clarinet Carina was doodling around. This created an exponential game of tops, pushing one another into new frenzies of energy. Feet in the humid warm humus of biological soil, squash vines all vibrant buzzing. It wasn't long before this function of energy in sound, began to become a function of bodies, two became four became eight became twenty five, and the second lines of guinea pigs, streaming into the hallways where the Carina's could not even see the floors or most walls, a sweaty moving patchwork carpet of multi-colored furs. Smoke filled the alleys and hallways. The smell of alcohol. Sound was an intense spectrum of light all around. The percussion! The horns!

'A File Marked Silence'

At first there was a bright white light like a ray of the sun. It fell upon the crystal around her neck and threw rainbows across the dark stone walls. She kept what she believed were her first memories close to her, if a time came when she was ever ready to proceed again down those beams. She had no glimmer as to the contents but would fondle the edges of the crystal, as if in prayer to some near collision of particles she had yet to face, the cold rock, all the childhoods and laughter, some from right after the grand spectacle, before all those islanders organized.

"Velma."

"What is it Carnelian?"

"The mines have misfortuned another encounter from the Isle of Flowers."

"And my soldiers on the great Tennissippi Lake?"

"No word. Your advisors have requested your council."

Velma loaded the hologram center. Columns of plasma,

inarticulate patterns in those crossover crystals, compression, and a bodily sensation of dissolution before that soft sound and a coming into focus of those boresome legalistic lots she hired more as a buffer to the public, a mediary between her and the consumers, rather than hosts to any insight. She needed their wall, the people could be so unjust, when times were good and there was a surplus she lost credits, but forbid if she didn't adjust her prices in famine. It was unfair.

"Velma. The Pike vein mines are completely buried and contaminated. The insurgents blew up our Fusion Plant on-site, the casualties are phenomenal."

"I'm certain you're aware this was our last active crystal vein that had plentiful..."

"We have lost all of our figures for this season. The backlog of applicants must be dealt with."

"We can't raise prices as per your proposal or things will just get worse."

"And the synthetic research is no where near..."

"Bad news, bad news. Come now, we are in the business of energy. So preserve me from these apocalyptic daydreams and lets talk about action. We have to strike back, the islanders are primitive rock throwers and we control the great center. Let's send another raid to the Palatka Island chain. Kill all known insurgents. Scorch the earth."

"That would be bad press, and concerning their progress in international food production, ill-advisable. We need to lower the cost of storage and preservation across the board by twenty percent. It would end these sentiments."

"There's a particular law of signs you fools don't understand. If something bad happens, you don't deal with it by giving something good to the transgressors, the result is negative. The only way to turn a negative into a positive is to multiply it by another negative. Simple mathematics."

...

The gourd craft unfurled its sail, it's fabric emptiness becoming full with the wind, catching the sun, shooting off electrons down copper cords, the onboard electronics hummed alive. Daphne guided her rudder south, the currents in the Great River were stronger than usual, she wondered if the other gourd crafts had made it out of the melee. The microwave uplinks were silent, but she loaded a coded beacon cue, taking care to hide her message in a standard tidal river report. Daphne was a few hours out from the archipelago of Old New Orleans, if the wind held and she was able to reserve power, she would be there soon. Crawfish and red beans, slunk off to some dark corner and wait to see if the others got out safely. Diane was down in the cargo hold. She had cried herself to sleep. She was new to the excursions. Daphne was worried about her, Diane sympathized too much. Death made her visibly shake. Daphne fondled the pearls upon her neck, mnemonically touching them with a strong prayer to the ocean deep.

"Daphne. The energy storage units aren't holding their optimal capacity."

"They must've been damaged in the explosions. I noticed our

astrological unit was out."

"Daphne. I don't like war. It doesn't feel right."

"You don't have to like it. It's ok."

"When we get to Old New Orleans can I speak to Mimi, I need to ask her something."

"It should be safe."

Daphne remembers the first time she left the Isleños. She was young and dumb. Wasted a few years of her life in Old New Orleans, brain cells blitzed and logic units lampooned, it was a fevered mad dream of moist forgetting, concrete and old architecture, diverse domains of sound and light, the floating exiles and their reed grass villages, atolls of colorful matrices of scrap, such music and people; like imbibed spirits, the intoxicating whirl of a history alive. She remembers the taletellers on the shell mounds, their wrinkled old hands shaking through white hazed eyes, vague glimpses of times before now, when there used to be land, and no one spoke about half-life and cell destruction; and eternity was a belief that got you through the day, not a threat of imprisonment.

...

"Mimi, I can't do this. I just want to be a gourd grower."

"Oh, warrior. The great Mutter Oshun said you must help fight the mainlanders. I know it's hard, but like calm sulphur burp from reed grass muck, and catfish god breathing air, strength is inside you."

"I don't want to hurt people. I miss the smell of dirt and the feel of fruit on vines. I dream I'm a waterbug and when I wake up I'm in a nightmare. All I do is think about getting back to sleep, the freedom of wings, seaweed on my face, I can't be a part of all this death."

"Oh, warrior. If the mainlanders aren't stopped they'll poison all the waters and then there would be no life to fill the veins of our plants. Their consumption knows no limits. How many islands? Crystal tortures?"

...

Daphne moored the gourd craft on the ocean side of Old New Orleans. She heard the sound of horns and percussion like the smell of home. Everything always changed here, but it also stayed the same, she felt a familiar fresh buzzing inside her chest, a vitality that she always thought would die but never did, such hope amidst realities white crests of wave. Clouds burst open with water parades down the canals of the city, riverboats buoyant and wail, it was like she had never left. She took the dinghy pad toward the swelter of sound, the smell of seafood and spice wafting about, bourbon lips and brightly costumed povertous decadents, she headed for her old haunt the Wooden Horse Saloon to get some food and the inevitable chance encounter of old or new lovers.

Here in Old New Orleans, amongst the infinite variations of the absurd denizen who found themselves amidst the cities mythic screams, and a chance encounter with another Flower Islander from the Palatka chains, eyes of water, silver tattoo on her lips, the salty sip of ocean. Her name was Kali and she was Daphne's first love. They'd drift off on lily pads in arms and tangled thighs at night under the stars, Kali would tell her rumors of faraway planets.

"That's the milky way. It's home to planets of only women. The great Mother Oshun made that star cluster from the milk of her breast, she needed a place for her children to sleep safely after all the bombs. They left the Isleños in giant gourds that moved through the sky with fire."

"Only women. How delightful... how dreamy...Lets run away."

"I can't. There's too much... I'm plagued with the threat of suspension, I couldn't let that happen to you... too much."

"I don't care! I thought I was just backwater crab tapping and afraid of the future... I have to. I must."

...

The Wooden Horse was the same school of barfish underwater goggling, glasses of grog. Dark hazy corners, tobacco smoke wove with other types of vapor tapestries across the ceiling. Daphne didn't recognize any faces; but they were all familiar. She took a stool, prominent in the middle of the bartop, opening herself to conversing.

"What'll it be babe?"

"A Shriek in Arabi, make it a double."

"Excuse me miss, me and my esteemed colleague have an informal bet. Could I please bother you for a second."

"Sure, hows it going."

"Swell, I'm Helen and this is Bernie. Bernie is under the assumption that the world is all an illusion and we are suspended in crystals already, and our cognition is just a logic program uploaded through the center."

"I'm not saying that's what I believe, Helen. It's just how would we know."

"Well, our bet is, if we were in such a logic program, and you became aware of it, would it effect your actions?"

"I don't think I could ever be certain, I guess."

"But what if you were."

"This is a silly bet."

"We're silly people. Bernie and I are scientists of sorts."

"Pseudo-scientists, she means."

"We are working on a technology for extracting electricity from clouds. At first we were using masers, and large transformer coils. Now we're focused on Ultraviolet lasers."

"Why? Roasted cloud trout?"

"Only unintentional, I assure you."

"We did eat a pelican once that we accidentally zapped."

"How horrible."

"It was gamey, not particularly the greatest dinner."

"Well, we're just trying to recreate a controlled setting of electric discharge, we figure one could make an ionized air tunnel using some sort of focused pathway. Our theory is sound."

"Whatever for?"

"An alternative to crystalline technology. The only way to change anything is to make it obsolete. Make something better, safer; this would be accessible to everyone, every person their own power plant. The decentralization of electricity. Perhaps the most revolutionary thing one could do."

"I don't know about that. It's like that time I saw that pack of water pigs flying in V formation."

"Hmmm, yes."

"Perhaps, this is part of your logic program, an absurd task that has no resolution, but a distraction to keep you busy for your crystal eternity."

"Hmmm..."

"I don't mean to offend, but there are some people who are actually fighting, giving up their life, to end the mainlanders destruction of the earth."

"Talking of water pigs at flight! Just like the invention of the guillotine by the esteemed Dr. Guillotine, an inventor of yore,

whom Bernie found out about. He created a stage for the old
revolutions spoken of in the symbol texts in the archives, he
created a tool that was a theater, this theater of decapitation
existed because of his set; inventions and technology, tools, are
the things that got us into these situations, and the only means
out. Studying electromagnetism is more revolutionary than
killing the infinitely headed hydra of soldiers."

"A new stage, one with confetti and noisemakers and spirits
and..."

"You must certainly believe yourself to be in a logic program,
your ego is very individualistic."

...

"That was peculiar. I think I drank too much Bernie."

"Look there's Helen, chasing clouds. Let's go home."

"Bernie, it's like wearing underwear. Sure it helps, but just keep
you pants washed, you know?"

"I don't know... Hey, what's that?"

Across the way on the docks, a far stumbling drunken way from
the Wooden Horse, two figures shaded in shadows by the moon,
carried a body into the port of a sub-ocean vehicle, lowering the
limp body down, and then disappearing into the waves.

"Just the smell of Old New Orleans, pirates abound, Bernie.
That's why I should abstain from getting so drunk."

"I don't feel good. Let's hurry home."

…

Diane with her fingers in the sand, digging for calm root, or off climbing a tree to harvest its mind cleanse cabbage, would have vague flashes of a memory of some other life. Her eyes would become static at night as she watched the rainbow fractals of the stars, or a soft luminescence from the carbon chimneys in the distance, she didn't remember when they were put there, or when the touch of water, instead of feeling pleasurable, felt awful. Did it used to feel good?

A whispering voice in the back of her throat kept saying, "Hey, what's going on."

"She seems to be stable."

Diane laying on the shore in the electric smog, dipped her hand into the water. It tingled, buzzed discomfort, like electric stones that would change size with the tide, the pain felt like it should have created awful visual bruises, to remind her, but nothing of the sort. She would always return to the calm root patch. It would distract her from that memory.

Up through the rafters of the giant grasses that she would weave into balloons for filling the skies with miraculous spectacles of fire that she would release at night as she huddled over a bowl of calm root and a digital warmth, a buzz of high frequency currents.

She seemed to be content that whatever sense of danger she used to feel was no longer around, if only she could remember what it was. There was a crystalline crevice in the center of her island. She would stare into it and maybe remember being a child, her hands were much smaller then. She remembered the gourds being much bigger, almost big enough to climb into. Her gourds now grew to the size of her foot and then rotted back into the ground, she had to depend on the bark of sleeping bush to make her bread. She would stare into the burning embers of the sky.

On a ruby aired fog, Diane felt like she was being watched.

"Hey Diane, did you see that valley of opiate creosote by the rolling silver sands, that plant has ancient stories, and such wondrous odors!"

"Oh, Velma? You're here? I thought..."

"Of course Diane. I was out collecting these forget me fruits! Such delicately candied exclamation points! How is your head feeling?"

"Oh, not good Velma. I don't feel good. I need some more calm root. My body needs it extensively. And I want to feel the sun. It touches me with such a sterile glare. I don't understand what is happening? Where is? Where is Mimi?"

"Oh poor child, you must still be sick, here is some calm root and eat these forget me fruits. I have this blackout beverage, take a sip. There breathe slow."

The array of matrix patches for sky, Diane could not feel her body, all she could think about was to go up the hill where she could see the smoke stacks and the red storied grasses and the desert of black glass shards, and with uncontrolled frenzy dig around for more calm root, which her teeth would lust while her tongue would sweat. She had a vague ghost recollection of throwing her body with unbreakable despair onto the sharp knife blades of the desert of black glass, thrashing against gravity as her body was cut apart, but then, or was it a dream, all the calm root and forget me fruits Diane could not tell, she didn't remember the last time Velma had came to her camp, they had discussed the astrological unit that mapped out a grid into the stories of the stars. Diane knew the stories well, she couldn't remember where she heard them but, the story of Atlatlatlatl the water snake that dipped down from the shores of Old New Orleans, and followed the graveyards of metals towards where the sun rises, but below it, and this snake Atlatlatlatl, with a skin harder than time-bombs that scrap apart the streams of Palatkas outer defense walls, but this is where she became forgetful again.

"Please Diane, we've gone over this like a fine toothed urchin eye. We have to know the defenses of the Isleños compound. They want us to die slowly, strangle us, take away our calm root, steal our thoughts to create their rich empires of electric resonance. Think hard Diane. I need your help."

A moving static wall of light and motion shuffled across the way, the sand became a frozen image, a mica strewn pixelated grey sound, Diane tried to draw the map for what seemed like an awful dream that kept up the steady repetition of demanding places and locations, "Here breathe calmly, I know this hurts, it's because you no longer have a body, shh..."

"Velma, I have an awful dreaded cavern in me. It feels like I am death."

Velma sat with a tree blade peeling the skin off of Diane's body, starting at her toes, on up to her face.

Diane would furiously cry rubbing her body raw in a vacant stared search for calm root. "I want to return to where the sky doesn't act like this. I can't remember the last time I felt the song of the earth. Didn't I hear it always before? Don't you know what I'm talking about Velma? The silent book that all us islanders are scribes to, and communicate with the songs of water, or the smell of Mimi as she would shelter me from rain, but ohh Velma! I remember rain! Do you remember rain Velma? I have a terrible feeling something wrong has happened."

"It has Diane, you are only data now, and we have to solve this problem because that is what data does."

It was an awful feeling that didn't last. She would watch the glitches of light splatter across the spaces where the scars should've been to record all the times Diane came to a certain gradience of realization to the situation, but beyond the fractions of light, dividing and pulsing, sending organizations of thought, into spaces that had the praying smell of colors, or she would remember future moments of great destruction that hadn't happened yet. After her millionth realization of her incorporeal nature, and life having not always been so, she began to devise a method of recording thoughts that wouldn't dissolve into the stream that ran through the island and into the crystalline orifice in its center washing away everything.

Diane would make slight changes to the gravity chambers that recoiled and fired off thought, and she knew Velma couldn't tell the slight differences. Velma couldn't read them like Diane could. Diane began to transcribe every thought in a delicate dance of gravity.

...

Bernie and Helen were watching the traffic glittering across the waters from the city, entertaining a stiff drink and an emboldened conversation on the recent Old New Orleans Tribune headline, 'Seacow Mutilations Strike Terror.'

"When I was a kid, we'd just roll em on their bellies until they passed out."

"You'd what?"

"You never did that?"

"No, thats awful."

"Well, at least we wouldn't mutilate them for youthful surgical excursions."

"It's not the kids, Bern."

"Oh don't bring that up again."

"It's just that wise crone with the shaggy cluster canopy said it was all those old time rituals back before the Islands in the days of the one continent. It makes sense. Kids don't make sense."

"Tell me how it makes sense that these sea cow mutilations are actually rips in the space-time fabric from all those old myth-texts that speak of ritual sacrifice. As if somehow killing a sea cow a million years ago in the name of some forgotten deity, could reach through to today."

"Supposedly Tanika over at the Drunken Moon had a friend who knew the lady who ran the Archive of Old Symbols and she said that there is a collection of old fragments that describe flying circles and beams of light and sea cow mutilations, and these correspond with space-time rips. Along with radiation and viral body infections. Time has more holes than a blarge fish has stomachs!"

"Excuse me, Old New Orleans Peoples Guard, we have a few questions for you two."

"See Bern, I told you that this kind of talk gets us in trouble, listen guards, we are just enjoying ourselves in ever glorious moderation in this sunlit shimmer of a grand damn day. We ain't pirates or politics. Just wet whistled scientists discussing the arcane matters of sea cow mutilation and the hallucinating responses of explanation thereof. See, my esteemed colleague proposes that these instances are in fact..."

"Please come with us. We have to perform symbol-temporal retrieval recordings on the two of you in relation to an occurrence last night. We think you may have seen something important."

"Here we go Helen, plump fortune waves her salty fins."

"At least its not that damned diet program you signed us up for last year! Seriously, Bernie, silicon is obviously not a proper food."

...

Daphne watched Bernie and Helen from behind the camouflage

of the mirror bush. They were recounting the shadow puppet recollection of a body being lowered into the submersible vessel. Their memories imprinting the view screens hazy recollect function, detailing craft identifiers.

"That must've been Diane, at the Dorgenois Docks, see, past there, the two of them went down there after I encountered them at the Wooden Horse. Dammit."

"You know that... You know Diane is probably..."

"Shut up Yamasee! Maybe it wasn't Velma. Maybe... I don't know what to do."

"She's probably already disembodied. We have to counter an attack, Diane knew a lot and she was young."

Daphne became a boiling weightless stream of magma veins, fists becoming marble, she wanted to explode with an atomic devastation and deed gifts to Oshun of herself confetti. She started to calculate the distance and incorporating the wind predictions, she consulted her astrological unit, fighting back temptations to continue multiple readings, the interface became aglow with the numbers, the statistical margins were uncomfortable, but she had already begun to unfold her additional sails from drydock, doing an electro-cellular status update.

Daphne sat on a shell mound a mile or so away from Old New Orleans, watching the haze of the city aglow like a flame dancing with vigorous rhythms of its occupants on ocean platform and the waters below, briny waves mirroring the visual sines of that dixie jass, skeletons in shells and sand like chemicals bonding, quartz chains of bones. The fibrous hull of her gourd craft bobbed and bubbled. Daphne wasn't all too sure she realized what was happening but was double checking her sail setup, disassembled and cleaned her fracture harpoon, accounted for inventories of explosives and arsenals and saw less and less hope as the poison gas knifes and jelly death spray bombs stacked up like patches of foreboding, finding switches in soft asides of weakness and terror she could let no one observe, or else things would become all too real.

...

Diane had found and duplicated a variety of calm root that was denser with matter, she had discovered a way to bypass the uptake of the alkaloidal effects, realizing she was no longer biological, instead consuming calm root in an exponential pattern of the addict while balling up the dense pouches of gravity inside her, playing around with their sizes and abilities, she had figured out a way to stretch the time between visits from Velma, without arousing suspension, by eating a variety of forget me fruit that she had modified with great center density allowing for increased perception times infinitely faster, slowing the extension Velma was party to, almost halting it.

She realized one day that as she was laughing at her crystalline predicament during her second burst of "Ha!" She relived an entire year on the Isleños, slipping around through the snake grasses of youth, the gurgling mud holes that'd suck you down and then shoot you up in the air like a rainbow bird, hollering all the way. The smell of sulphur as the women would sponge each other at the sacred springs. The bells and songs of youth! She didn't want to leave, she was enjoying the tide of memory uncovering those forgotten smells.

She had transcribed enough to gravity to reveal her situation, plus a few memories that were not her own. They were on a layer of gravity she was just starting to explore, she had to ball up all her roots and fruits into one hot spot of light, to begin to glimpse these other layers, but she was starting to see there was so much more than she first thought.

...

Carnelian moved swiftly down the corridor and shut the terrace barriers with haste as she loaded the hologram center. "Send update to file marked 'silence'. Things have begun to look precarious for the Pike Mine Energy operations. Perhaps let this and previous updates reference the aberrant software of Velma. Velma seems to have regained the crystal that disappeared from the archive containing her histories. Let the advisors be aware of these factors. Also, she seems to be disappearing into a crystal program that she has been working on for a while. We are unaware of it's function. More research is necessary." Carnelian recalibrated the cache system of her recall, to partition this experience from sight of Velma and examined a matrix of associations and charts of planetary random elements that she would choreograph for some sort of insight into the matter, creating a report for the advisors.

...

Diane found herself in a crystalline palace of her own design deep at the densest points. A fractaling biomorphic pleasure dome, floating in a space that was dripping in all points of time at once, she could feel her mothers and her mothers mothers heart beat to fiery rows of delight, or further away, but yet closer than a pulse of kelp light, she saw metal skeleton buildings beaming of sight, old architecture of columns, fabled cities of smokey lore with their infinite peoples, she joined in on celebrations of color, festivals of such music, amid sour histories ebb of tragedy.

"I am aware of my molecules to an infinite degree, breathe."

She went down to her island, dancing through her transcribed histories in gravity, imagining her lungs to fill with such pleasant air, a sweat laden brow, muscles in thighs vibrant to her patterns of intricate step. Diane saw Velma gathering herbs for entropic memory tea amid the neon growth of spring flowers. She watched Velma without enmity, almost overcome with sadness viewing her like a dance of channeling that stuck roots deep into the sad earth and its horrible bones and the blood memories and these were re-enacted in the movements of her hands and legs.

"Velma, I know I am no longer Diane."

"Diane, where'd you come from? I was about to..."

"The crystalline network and the gravities of time! Have you seen the sun rise while volcanoes explode and this planet we inhabit, these electric oceans of such glorious mythological waves, gourd craft and all become fiery dust, like my own decomposing body in your time, it comes to an end. But the crystals! Not to mention the dances of gravity and their own glorious myths!"

...

Sail unfurled in radiant networks of light, charging storage units, and propelling Daphne's gourd craft upstream, the muscles in her forearms tight, as she adjusted lines and tensions, measuring the waters temperature, watching flocks of gloom birds, weighing all strategies and outcomes with a studied patience, mounted atop a war cry of gourd craft barreling against the Great River's current.

They had rallied a large front and were insistent upon a direct assault to Ice Lake vaults. This is where Diane's consciousness would've been imprisoned. They were going to destroy the compound.

...

Diane gently presented Velma memories vast architecture from a childhood, they danced off amongst the reed grass and goat bugs of the Flowers and the Islands, they swung from purple fleshy vines into livid streams splash, they tucked their toes in the salt fields of verdure hot springs, precipitating up from a rubicund solution of liquid, through which she could finally begin to uncover the elaborate gestures through gravity that were new ways of experiencing that she could barely believe but was excited for the great game of play.

...

Carnelian moved swiftly, loaded the hologram center, "Immediate updates to file marked 'Silence'. Velma has loaded into the crystal she stole from the archives. Velma is no longer. There is a sizable fleet of Isle of Flowers insurgents headed to the Ice Factory Number 237, it is to be abandoned."

'A Bicycle Named Perseverance'

President Donald Trump reportedly grew enraged at a June meeting over the amount of visas awarded to travelers from certain countries, grumbling that 15,000 Haitians who entered the United States in the preceding months "all have AIDS" and that the 40,000 Nigerian visitors would never "go back to their huts" in Africa.{{1}}

When Trump lost all of his body hair and had been poisoned, his glands altered, ballooning his flesh out, tears would fall out of his jellied eyes and moisten the curves and folds, mucusoidal strings, yellow liverish ballooning flesh, tears would fall out like jelly in the curves of his dark yellow liverish mucusoidal flesh. Sucking in oxygen where a nose used to be like a childs play toy in a swimming pool.

When Trump lost all of his body hair from the mucusoidal genetic alteration, from the ballooning spacecraft where he was taken and subsequently lost all of his body hair. All of the television viewing public watched as Trump was taken up into the balloon-like spacecraft, you could see on his face as it was happening, you could see on his face he was in over his head, he was in over his head on his face, it was terrifying how you could see it on him.

Andrew Jackson was paranoid and thought all the ghosts were finally fulfilling vengeance oaths. All of the ghosts were going to kill him. Andrew Jackson filled with fear and paranoia hid under his blankets crying, because the ghosts were coming to kill him, it was certain. "No matter how much you burn that Copal, I don't think it will help."

"Anyways Andrew, you're clouding up the space port, we have a schematic of flights that must hold to schedule."

The bicycle named Perseverance. Written with thick dark paint.

The Marine Corps commandant told about 300 Marines in Norway this week that they should be prepared for a "bigass fight" to come, remarks his spokesman later said were not in reference to any specific adversary but rather intended to inspire the troops.

"I hope I'm wrong, but there's a war coming," Gen. Robert Neller told the Marines on Thursday, according to Military.com. "You're in a fight here, an informational fight, a political fight, by your presence."{{2}}

Andrew Jackson pulled the fleshy mass of hairless jelly that was Donald Trump in a radio flyer wagon around the Central Business District of New Orleans, they stood at One Shell Square admiring the size.

"Andrew, I want to go back to Bourbon street. I feel alive there. No one looks at me like a fleshy mass, they don't look at me at all."

"And of the Mardi Gras Donald? What of the Mardi Gras?"

"High Geared."

Andrew Jackson with tired exasperation took rest from pulling the radio flyer wagon that contained the fleshy mass of bulbous glob that was Donald Trump, up and down the streets and alleys and curves of the Central Business District of New Orleans. "I'm writing a book about the architecture of early millennial parking garages in the CBD. It's sort of a coffee table kind of thing. Andrew on Architecture. A whole series. The millennials and their gaze."

"Andrew, I want to go back to Bourbon street!"

"I will leave you here if you don't cool it. What do you think of this Breaking Away poster?"

Andrew Jackson wheeled Donald Trump with aplomb amusement past burning trash cans and abandoned cars, dripping plastic fairing like mascara through tears, and the steadily dying whine of the horn aflame. Andrew Jackson wasn't happy to be back in New Orleans. "Too many kids running around without knowing anything about history. The kids these days! Back in my day..."

"There he goes." Ever since his encounter with the aliens on the space craft where Donald Trump lost all of the hair on his body and ballooning without recourse to cessate, his entire mucusoidal genetics had been altered, there were no bones left in his hairless body, like a liquid he took the shape of his container, which currently was a red radio flyer wagon that Andrew Jackson pulled through the Central Business District of

New Orleans.

Andrew Jackson on the Natchez Trace Parkway maneuvering a recumbent. The red radio flyer of the altered mucusoidal genetics of the hairless and boneless Donald Trump who took the shape of the container that he found himself inside. A Rectangle with curved edges. But sometimes, thin tubes like tentacles of fleshy mass strung from over the edge of the red radio flyer. Donald Trump would pretend to not feel embarrassed when this happened, but he had no control of the tubular stretches of fleshy mass that strung alongside the red radio flyer like tubes. Andrew Jackson took care of his recumbent bicycle that he had declared, "Perseverance! Perseverance!" Andrew Jackson well oiled and greased his recumbent bicycle named Perseverance. "To speak of the weather!" Andrew Jackson would declare upon the Natchez Trace.

Police said Stewart arrived at the Dublin post office around 4:30 a.m. -- three hours early -- approached Herrera-Dempsey, and shot him. When the supervisor fell to the floor, Stewart shot him again, killing him, police said.

About three hours later, Stewart – again naked and armed – was seen chasing postmaster Ginger Ballard, 53, around a parking lot, the Dispatch reported.

Then Stewart threw her to the ground, where she struck her head and died, according to police.{{3}}

"Psss Hey."

"You call?"

"Yeah, you Andrew Jackson, yeah, you got that bicycle perseverance, I see that, Yeah you got the fleshy mass of Donald Trump in a radio flyer wagon, I see that. You Andrew Jackson and it's a pleasure. Andrew Jackson got the bicycle perseverance. We're looking for someone like you."

"We are?"

"Yeah Babe. I need someone like you, we got this museum, theres this museum and we've been collecting all these taxidermied specimens, everything for these museums, its a federal project, everything is covered. There's rumor, a few days back I heard rumors of a pelican still alive out in the sludge of Bayou Bienvenue. Some industrial crawfish bacteria farmers, said they saw one, chased one away from their chemicals."

"A pelican? You say? Unicorns and talking starfish?"

"Monsieur, need not throw stones lest yr own glass house tumble shatter. The folly of living in a green house, no? The cost of economies of oxygen, no?"

"Disgusting moist. What are the terms? Of said pelican for taxidermy."

"So, you see, you must recognize the delicacy of this last pelican. Pelican's haven't been seen in years, this is most likely the very last Pelican to exist, self explanatory delicacy. Why we approached someone of your delicacies, if you can see the delicate nature."

Seven children were among the 20 killed on Christmas Day when a passenger jeepney collided with a bus here at 3:30 a.m.

along the southbound lane of the Manila North Road in
Barangay (village) San Jose Sur.

Six-month-old Kyle Cabagbag was the youngest fatality.{{4}}

"Andrew, Hey Andrew. Hey, listen to this. Andrew listen to this,
what if. Just hypothetically, but it would be a smart step in our
um...association, if we used the money from this pelican case to
get me an intergalactic gold bionic skeleton, right. Get rid of the
radio flyer, switch it up, just an idea, but the intergalactic gold
bionic skeletons could be fitted into my fleshy bulbous mass to
give it a rigid, um... most handsome structure. It would be a
good business move for our um...association."

"People are proud to be saying Merry Christmas again," Trump
tweeted. "I am proud to have led the charge against the assault
of our cherished and beautiful phrase. MERRY
CHRISTMAS!!!!!" {{5}}

Andrew Jackson left the radio flyer wagon containing Donald
Trump in front of a small stage in Jackson Square by a busking
puppeteer eating a cold fried kidney in December gravy, taking a
lunch break, sitting to the side of his theater and its sign
promising a performance in ten minutes, at which the fleshy
mass of Donald Trump heckled and gurgled inflammatory
bilious sayings, being promised by Andrew Jackson to one of the
best Punch and Judy acts in America right now. "Right here in
the French Quarter, our Trouble Making friend Punch, Is
assimilated into the New Orleans Vortex. Come One and All.
See the intellect and wit of Judy, as she..."

"Seriously, you know my adoration of Punch. You're not
messing with me, Andrew, are you messing with me? Seriously, I

adore Punch. They have the gator? Or the devil? Gator or devil?"

"Donald, you have no patience. They have both the gator and the devil. Wait here and watch this, I'll be back, I gotta talk to someone."

The geometric caverns of the lower Mississippi, the mathematic delta myth. "Catedral de San Luis."

"And the pleasure gardens of the Square, beyond that, the river."

"The people's theater all around. I've decided to take on a job."

"Flags and Chandeliers. Chandeliers and Flags."

"Mythic squiggling terror from the ceiling. All is alive. But these checkerboard floors! These checkerboard floors!"

"One full revolution of the pedals."

A topless protester was detained by Vatican police on Monday for attempting to steal the doll of baby Jesus from the Vatican's nativity scene. The incident occurred as thousands of people gathered in St. Peter's Square to hear the Pope's Christmas Day message. (...) The woman, identified by Femen as Ukrainian "sextremist" Alisa Vinogradova, had "God is Woman" written on her torso.{{6}}

"But it's just food coloring."

"Does the trick."

At least four Russian ships, including a warship and an

intelligence-gathering ship, passed near British waters starting on Saturday, the British Navy said. The traffic on the water meant British sailors on the Royal Navy frigate St. Albans spent Christmas tracking their Russian counterparts. {{7}}

"Something about a cathedral."

"Do you know about Li Po? The man who drinks with the moon and his shadow? Never lonely?"

"General Lee? Thought him well off? Robert E?"

"Flowers and wine! Wine and Flowers! Such things of beauty for passing horrors hours."

"I take it, this next bottle is to be had in honour?"

"Teeth and sprocket and chainring!"

"And the next! And the next! Be kind and tip some into my fiendish fleshy mass of a friend at your side, he needs juice just like us skeletal folk do."

"Sexuality!"

They could make fires on the batture at night, drinking with the mosquitoes shiver, no one would bother them there, on a peninsula of mud sludge, the Mississippi maelstrom, throwing bones like dice down river, "Double or nothing."

"That means you drink two, ahhhh."

"Double or nothing. Double or nothing."

"Gear ratios!"

Donald Trump, in a perpetual fleshy mass bulbous form, a coming-to from the night before, trying to stretch his fingers in painful joy, or to shift side to side on his spine, to move anything … found nothing, no sensation of self, but the puddle, the shape of a radio flyer, waking up again. He would find himself in motion. Having no command to steer, being merely the contents of a red shiny radio flyer wagon. A fleshy mass of skin and organs with mouth and eye flaps floating on top, the rest a puddled swamp of folds or tubular rounds, or squishy glandular nodules.

"Lots of oil. So much oil."

(…) the stately evergreen was brought to Washington as a seedling by Andrew Jackson. The magnolia was a favorite tree of his wife, Rachel, who had died just days after he was elected. Jackson blamed the vicious campaign — during which his political opponents questioned the legitimacy of his marriage — for his wife's untimely death.

Someday, Grantham would like to bring a cutting, or an exact clone, of the White House magnolia back to the Hermitage. "I know there are some out there," he said. In those trees, Jackson's two-century-old tribute lives on.{{8}}

"The socialite Ellen Glasgow of Richmond history. Her Richmond doesn't exist. And of the witch Elizabeth Van Lew? A Richmond that no longer exists, but will of course always exist."

"Or the mob of the Democratic party, smashing through the doors, foaming cream pimples hate. Daft lot whole. Terrifying to be near a mob. Terrifying. Without disguise, they openly took arm against the police and military. And Pinchback's frustration!"

"Time creates some mad brew. Jean Toomer in New England studying in a Gurdjieff group."

"Louise De Mortie, Papa Laine, Black Benny, Sidney Bechet's grandfather Omar."

"Manuel Perez."

Students were among those who had gathered at the Shia centre for a discussion forum.

The interior ministry said the event was to mark the 38th anniversary of the Soviet invasion of Afghanistan.

Another witness, Sayed Jan, told reporters from his hospital bed: "There was a book reading event and academic discussion, and I was one of the participants. During the speech a huge bang was heard and smoke rose from inside the hall.

"My face was burning. I fell down from the chair and I saw the other colleagues around me on the ground. The smoke was everywhere."{{9}}

"So we are in agreement?"

"We'll go to the tapas place to celebrate. Small plates!"

"Should we sign the documents?"

"And the growlers of cold brew coffee? Or sassafras candies? Peanut brittle, pine bark chips, dried crickets in cacao powder, ionic gold liquor dates, warm caramels of golden seal, fresh cream."

"And of your equity?"

"I want my endoskeleton to be coated lavender and coltsfoot. Like a bee at the sea forest rotten with mammals milk."

"A sex worker?"

No one could hear him over the rattle of the radio flyer wagon on the brick streets.

"They were setting up a generator show on the levee. Riverboats passing by."

"Kids living like ghosts in abandoned houses fueled by lsd and beer."

"Kids living like ghosts eating garbage for the worms in their bodies to stay warm."

"That time Andrew Jackson horrendously brought that poor dead giant pelican to the punk show, three to four foot tall, wingspan just as engulfing, the limp giant body, lifeless, slung about the sweaty throng in a slurred thrash. I was drinking wine coolers, I can't handle gluten. Not right for me, no thank you. No beer. Lots of wine coolers, and that dead limp giant pelican, I was always fractured gross."

"A cold winter's celebration. Kids in lead attic. Kids in slime wood box. Breathing in the moist moldy, sure enough, all those metal shards."

"Kids on trains with body-cameras-live-streaming their journeys south on abandoned conductors throne."

"Kids with moldy body rash on mattress on neutral ground, streamers exploding in their hands smoke filled the street lungs."

Zackari Parrish, a 29-year-old deputy, died Sunday morning, while four other officers were injured. Authorities have released few details about what transpired inside an apartment unit in Highlands Ranch, Colo., a few miles south of Denver, where Parrish and the others responded after receiving a noise complaint. But Douglas County Sheriff Tony Spurlock described the shooting as "an ambush-type attack on our officers."{{10}}

Andrew Jackson, big kids playground, Andrew Jackson and the Bad Kids Club, Andrew Jackson capricious gander, Andrew Jackson, the bard of lower Decatur, "Takin' drugs that used to work, but no longer do./ At Barracks and Decatur/ hexagonal tile/ red brick not yet crushed up for voodoo. / Point in Glass, some old concussion, bundled up, but sending rays, twenty one of them, outwards/ bursts/ Saint Cecilia, Hildegard von Bingen/ Joan D'arc, Saint Roch.

"New Years Eve and four yule/ wreaths hung in domed windows of red brick. Glossy pine. Plastic red and plastic gold.

"The black Rubber from the Wheel of a Carriage hanging on Air Conditioner Window Unit.

"Bicycles shackled to Balcony Poles.

"A two basin aluminum sink/ one rectangular becrumbed and sodden baking pan./ One circular baking pan./ Soiled utensils, plastic/ Mardi Gras cups and glass/ mason jars, smudged/ and soiled, a wet/ hand towel quartered,/ clean and calcined/ dish racks,/ black eyed peas soaking/ water and salt for tomorrow/ a circular cigarette tray, like a fine sunny beach of ash/ rolled cigarette ends like towels/ and bodies."

He listened to the church bells like car horns of irate pilots. Amen.

The United States is "closer to a nuclear war with North Korea" than ever before, Adm. Mike Mullen, a former chairman of the Joint Chiefs of Staff, said Sunday, adding that he does not "see the opportunities to solve this diplomatically at this particular point."{{11}}

The attacker set off an explosive vest among mourners gathered for the funeral of Gul Wali, the former district chief of Haskah Menah, according to Attaullah Khogyani, a spokesman for the governor of Nangarhar Province.{{12}}

Onlookers and passersby, bundled up against the damp, year-ending cold, smiled and danced to the music as the Rollers made their way through Central City. The group was scheduled to also take a moment of silence in memory of Mansfield "Field" Patterson III.{{13}}

"It's a full Cancer moon."

"...or the hexagram, 'Preponderance of the Great.' Sagging ridge pole. Water goes over my head."

"Or flipping over one card... the fool. The bright yellow sun, flower in bloom in palm, vagabond with starry cloth like feathers, small white dog exuberant like dwarf horse, eyes raised in romance at the cliffs edge, the fool."

"Or flipping another card, water crystal oracle...hope."

'The Adventures of Bleachy Viberts: Polytan Platinum and Beerlord Buttface Cajole Sleek Part 2'

Fifty rough cobblers press leathery index, swain and abrupt. "Here is the story! Here. Here." Crowing nightbirds with their calling hack and satellite eyes on procession. Fifty angled cobblers gathered sworn indexed inventories. "All the different arches!"

"Yes, and the brahman hide."

"And ... hide.
Tell me ... ride, the brahman
and ... the alligator."

"Twenty sumptuous cobblers, anglers all, laced up water boots."

"The damn bark of the curl owl. Beast of candida feast."

"Leaving thirty inquisitive cobblers?"

At the groundbreaking ceremony of Old Rivers Enterprise, an

industrious crew of alchemists, transmuting waterways to metal slag refuse, gathered up handshakes like souls.

The 10-pound benign tumor grew on Emanuel Zayas' face as a result from a condition called polyostotic fibrous dysplacia. The medical condition occurs when developmentally certain bones become soft. {{14}}

The gambling bells of the city in the moon. Cantos for the dead sizzling like fat back on the stone left out in the sun. The Oysters on the River's tumor. Gulfs of abscess. Oily veins spurt and exhaust. Severed like incandescent light on the redeye, Bleachy Viberts rescued a sense of declaration, "Certainly they must have toilettes."

Polytan Platinum a curious Philadelphian wore all black calling on Bleachy on a Saturday before Christmas. Polytan and Bleachy wore knit slack arms, slinging low down, sunsets pink, red, orange, purple, blue, black. Polytan snuggled Bleachy's parchment skills. "A canine. Should not be responded with 'BINGO'. For obvious tangibilities."

And so it was roomy chestnuts blighted roast, was laudanum and Andrew Jackson ever aloof, scattered tetanus points like grids. "Here, could we gather communications to the stars. Here. Here."

Bruce McCandless, who made first untethered space flight, dies at 80.

McCandless orbited at 18,000mph (29,000km/h), using a hefty jet pack to propel himself away from and then back towards the Space Shuttle.{{15}} "Kind of makes me nauseous," chuckled

Bleachy, quickly moving her hands away from the tentacles that instantaneously inhabited the space around Andrew Jackson, and he disappeared in a violent brush. "It's like Benjamin Franklin worship. Dionysus. Mickey Mouse. Fireworks and Machine guns."

What at first bothered Andrew Jackson was all the weight, to escape the disease of self immolation, all of Russia in flame, he'd carry 8kg of unpublished manuscripts through the ports of Mars, next to the ancient ruins of 'the face'. His total allowed weight was 12kg, he'd recall like a madman, shaking legs at the coldness, without a coat, trying to visualize a flame of crystal from the back of his spine on up through the hair top, and metal roofs tingling like rains song. On Mars where lurid accounts and gambling armies survived great roles. On Mars, they had developed uncommon identities of music. On Mars the barroom banquet halls aflame with intoxicated knives and body odors. On Mars they could survive great lurid gambling barroom banquet halls totally destroyed with crumpled metal chairs in a pool of green sludgy blood gurgling top.

Andrew Jackson with viral alarm in his voice, "They're selling genetically modified influenza on lower Decatur. Bleachy got some cabbage in the Teleport Slammer, where Bleachy ... uptown to the St Patricks Day parade ... next year three minutes ago, Bleachy emboldened, abruptly wept, snakes from her eyes like Ireland. Under roadways wiggling all worms, the great feast of wiggles. Queen Wiggles of Voluptuous Merit! Carnival wands glitter in storms!"

The Trump administration said Friday it will renew mining leases to extract copper and nickel adjacent to a Minnesota wilderness area, reversing an Obama administration decision

and giving a victory to a Chilean billionaire who is renting a
mansion to the family of the president's elder daughter. {{16}}

"And this talk of weather!"
"The weather, yes."
"The weather."
"Clouds and sun and rain."
"Yes, weather."

"The bells resonance in the air over Our Lady Star of the Sea.
The graveyards of Saint Roch."

Polytan with perjurous presence of self, shoes all lit up like fresh,
gathered a crowd of ears, "Therefore we gotta quit all this
nonsense, get smart, figure out the puzzles, and divulge the gold.
Get that silver. Prospectors … mineral flaked and buoyant."

"La la the king is dead, off with his head. La la the king is dead
… rivers red. Bodies..."

"Doing lines of pine tree pollen, feeding the mouths of fleshy
pores saw palmetto extract yellow number five."

"My dear Polytan that is no life for sailors. We need the foamy
electric death of endless stars and no hope for solid land, and
white squalls in all directions."

At the groundbreaking cloak of Old Runaways Enterprise,
Polytan stood towards the back, fondling his blasting iron in the
curve of his overcoat. Polytan was waiting for Andrew Jackson to
be escorted to the front, his grey hickory hairs like hordes of
thin worms erect to sunlight, shimmering with protest. Polytan
took aim.

Two grecian statues, the Indian Killer stood enraged with his cane lifted. A soft glow. Polytan kept pulling the trigger.

"King Richard did cause quite the scene at the Capitol."

"Not worth remark, what of the UFO's and green technology coverup? What of it?"

"I do think Missus Polytan Platinum has been sparingly vague on the occurrence."

"Verily so, I've slaughtered my klob stick, vulnerable a sense of clobbing the inevitable. Taking force straight on with a slobby kill arm."

The columns were very cinematic. To move behind, or peacocks alight downwind. "Not to even mention the bathhouse greenery."

"They have certain plants from South America."

"When the last capitalist is strung up from a lamp pole by the guts of the last oligarch!" Andrew Jackson would tirade through the French Quarter.

Ahmed Aminamin El-Mofty fired at a Harrisburg police officer on Friday afternoon and later at a state trooper, wounding her before pursuing her, Dauphin County District Attorney Ed Marsico said.

"He fired several shots at a Capitol police officer and at a Pennsylvania state police trooper in marked vehicles," Marsico told reporters, flanked by state police, Capitol police and FBI officials.{{17}}

Off from the murder towers of upper Tulane, past dusty cabbage alleys, gothic tabernacles of the Judge of Babylon, electric arcs, and hosiery disheveled, bullets fired towards the lake. The German ghosts sat under beer goblets of rudy tusk. The ideograms of burdock and oranges. Andrew Jackson laced curled toes.

The glandular sunset of square wave at the waterfront. Off behind us, there it goes behind the Disneyland, the pink princess party of smug Jazz men. Merrily go round the usury, all daisies push back. All of 1949 rolled up in pink princess party of jolly bankers. Off behind us, the square wave wall flowers incite pink princess party, too many words, "Sloppery, dabblegashed, gushing! Gushy!" Off in the murder fields above Broad, by the canal, where as children they saw their first floating bodies, almost the color blue. The old bridge that would swing across towards Gert Town. Momma would go after Grandma when she would walk across the old bridge that would swing across Carollton towards the music up against the river. A bottle of colored spirits, dyed caramel across the old bridge that would swing. In the water, they saw a glimpse of blue, like when they were children and they saw their first dead bodies floating, exposed to air, the cold morning blue. This was when there was a canal. "Yoruba, Yoruba." Andrew Jackson would turn on his Nintendo Sixty Four and wait for the cartridge to load.

"As part of our Christmas decoration, we would display the name Jesus to point out to everyone that we in this family believe that the reason for the season is to celebrate the birth of Jesus," said Mark Wivell told FOX43.

But the homeowner's association wasn't having it.{{18}} Bleachy

Viberts saddled up empty to the Ownership Runway Enterprises, breaking in the ground where she stood, waiting for the game to load she believed in her association. Bleachy could no longer disguise her agreeable nature towards the cobblers. She cared a lot about her feet. "When you look this good you have to care."

"Don't snort at me. It's just a badge, it's like a mask."

"I'm sure the rash is just temporary."

Marquise Byrd was sitting in the passenger seat of a vehicle traveling southbound on Interstate 75 Tuesday evening when he was struck by the construction sandbag, the Detroit Free Press reported. The driver, who was not injured, pulled over and then phoned 911.

"I don't know what happened, my friend, I don't know what happened he's not moving," she told the dispatcher.

"I was just driving underneath the bridge and something hit my car. He is not moving."{{19}} The humpbacked whale somersaulted through the water like the curves in an overpass, red lights trailing.

They couldn't tell the difference between a picture of New York City turned upside down, versus one with an upright stance. "It looks the same to me?"

"And what of the holes from meteors?"

"The geologic formations of limestone?"

"The orange and red along the Ganges?"

"Volcano cones filled with emerald grass."

"Big green animal friend dripping paint, making holes in the limestone like New York City."

Bleachy came to the French Quarter in a depressive submission to alcoholism. She shifted for appearances ... arm wrestling Beerlord Buttface for a dice game and a candy red corvette. Beerlord Buttface glazed with sweat, wished there were better ways to clean a carburetor that didn't require the drinking of so much ethanol.

Beerlord wished a glazed depressive alcohol sweat against the New York City rafters. A small studio in Flushing, storing hydrogen in old Diet Coke plastic bottles. Beerlord envious abrupt, shattered daylight with such self esteem and stamina, he could righteous uptake the drugs with pure hydrogen injected speed. Making water her mom would say. Beerlord whimpered a sensual tongue of air. Abruptly to New Orleans. Making eye at the houses of the moon and sun.

"Faubourg Sainte Marie! Sainte Marie! Wo Wohnen Sie! Wohnen Sie? Faubourg Ste Marie, wohnen sie?."

"I, Bleachy Viberts, filled with cancer and worms, do send a joyous squeal up into the rafters! A making-eye lust for life, abrupt self esteem, more drugs Beerlord, we need more intoxicants to get a closer glimpse of the..."

"I, Beerlord Buttface, inebriated and just so, to envelope the sound around me with a swift tongue, drinking more wine than air, coming ever closer to..."

The humpbacked whale doing somersaults like roadways upon roadways upon roadways upon...

Like Amazon's other smart speakers, the Echo Look will tell you the weather or play music. But the oval-shaped product also has a voice-controlled camera for taking photos of you in various outfits. It works alongside an app.

Related: Amazon's $200 Echo Look will judge your outfits

After snapping photos of you in two outfits in front of the device, its built-in Style Check tool decides which one is best. It leans on a combination of machine learning technology and human opinion. {{20}}

"And there were two sailboats filled with wind, surging against the rivers course."

"I don't think Andrew Jackson understands the intricacies of Noh."

"Old King Fentanyl gathered lazily silicon flowers of the Walmart valleys and aisles, the cold stethoscope, smell of washed hands. Old King Fentanyl gathers royal jelly for the feast. Old King Fentanyl gathering royal candies and song."

"The way Andrew Jackson designed the space colonies. Can you imagine the impact of the changes in ones biology? Floating in free flight, giving up bones."

Bleachy Viberts remembered the Federal case against them. Just as quickly she forgot it.

"Stop thinking about Twitter, Andrew!"

"I can't help, I have to look. Oh those damned..."

"Andrew! What is this of..."

"Seriously we must speak of phalanxes and contracts."

The perpetual crescendo of Schoenberg.

Bleachy Viberts tried to relax casual enough, but had been putting off...

'The Adventures of Bleachy Viberts: Bleachy and Beerlord Recount the Past Part 4'

Raw dogging in the space cover. His arms overthrown. Two small globular knobs. A radiant sweat pus pore. Grimey Cadillacs wired together to create a high voltage environment. When he was a child, they'd make antenna's from innumerable repurposed objects, "She said laying into the water, murmuring, yarrow, yarrow."

The buzz of the electrical frequency was a base tone in their musical system, Kodak would ensure to program the batteries voltage to irrational numbers, staying up late at night in cheap motels on the abandoned side of town, rubbing meth from his crime and punching numbers into a blue haze, "The square root of e minus the square root of negative one."

"Stop being such a square," Bleachy Viberts, slunked behind Kodak, holding his gun for him, adjusting the loud speaker they were using to communicate with the SWAT team outside. Bleachy would spin a sine wave and up the white noise to punctuate the comedic notions of armed warfare, as the tactical units swarmed the dark, automatic klob arms dripping.

Kodak waved ass at the rafters, "Ya damn rats! Rats!"

Bleachy Viberts holographed to Clobber Occupied Walmarket. "We have a dysfunction."

A room of geodesic shapes in chorus of flashing light that was both smell and taste and sound like a stream bending over a fallen tree cyborg.

"Has your doo doo butt ray collapsed intellectual property rights?"

"Has your poo poo pee pee capitalism gland popped?

"Have occult wee wee stock market cultural genocide?"

"Pee poop feed money mommy ma ma poo poo pa pa."

"Bleachy Viberts, columns of air and light!"

"Beerlord Buttface, full of grace and divine!"

"Bleachy Viberts, glory of sanctities macro-laser-hologram-network-data!"

"Beerlord Buttface, friend of the numerical lovesick!"

"My dear Bleachy, what is going on with you and Kodak."

"Beerlord Buttface, everything has gone wrong, it has to do with Kodak's developments in the irrational. At first he was all binary, into ones and zeroes, but he got into elaborate functions of self gratification, the mind loop, he's caught, glamored in bars, cages like Hollywood."

"And now you've got wet glubs slapping the rubber?"

"Yeah Beerlord, snail glubs in creosote nodules, I almost can't take in oxygen."

"Trapped within your world."

"Oh, I guess I get what you mean."

"At that moment, I Beerlord Buttface began a narration on the happenings of Bleachy Viberts in the following timelines, folded up like blankets so that different points touch, and the worn out holes of soft fabric. After Bleachy realized they were not 'trapped within their world.' They were in fact consisting of free will."

Bleachy returned to their apartment in Mayaguez Puerto Rico, leaning against the concrete brick walls for a cool length. Bleachy Viberts name tag, a rectangular data station, their DNA and quartz simulacra storage disk. Edit. Control. Kodak and Andrew Jackson were ransoming reason to an experiment involving overpass demolition.

"I told you self implosion was fairly simple," a passerby said they had heard Andrew Jackson scream at Kodak as they ran off. Andrew Jackson wore a synth gland controller under a breast scar that stayed waxy and grew no hair. Bleachy would lay on the beach.

Two small piezo wild hover cats frolicked about amidst the sand, their silicon in the sun. There was a heavy metal and radiation waste pool they would instantly recall joyously, recollect loops, calendars Bleachy would mark with strings of words and associated events. The piezo wild hover cats pizza showered Bleachy.

"Cute pets Bleachy. How long you gonna live this life? This time?"

"As long as I need."

Bleachy would record to the minute pulls of gravity in objects, a new data storage system devised by Andrew Jackson on a blurb overdose, photographs and film segments, that Bleachy would tell locals, "It's a short film. A documentary I'm working on about the grey bodied beings that are everywhere."

"La gris gris!"

Andrew Jackson and Bleachy would recount a recollection when they exchanged sexes, and forgot who was who. Andrew deemed flesh immaterial and uploaded time chips on the being port. Bleachy would melt their skin together in a hijack virus data chain, they would become an island off the coast of Africa millions of years ago, peopled by a population of rogue strings, rainbowed flaps of wind, the most spectacular vistas of dry red and purples and endless stretching into skies, dust tornadoes marble roving data flesh robots. Kodak in a fit of jealousy marketed desire. Desire no longer could afford the infomercials, General Lee was charging too much, and the Osceola mascots of foam and cotton adrift in the graves.

General Lee flumoxed with Andrew Jacksons makeup cordials, became lit with the sensation of jovial pranksterism. General Lee rewrote his DNA with a text file, and patched express the links to different historical spaces inside spaces, cupping General Lee's nipples to fleshy lips, sunburned and battered, they would empty space trucks of waste and create vibrant forests through the blood summers. Bleachy and General Lee sat out on the intergalactic docks south of the University of Mayaguez, near the old town square, jostling papers CointelPro and Microsoft Paint faxes.

General Lee whispered into Andrew Jackson's ear, "Velvet remorse, can you read the pulses of the blood pumping in my wrist, I think it's a code, but I don't understand that high of bit."

Andrew Jackson wrapped General Lee's bird like arm under his chin, bending down with data, Beerlord gathered a row of sound, the space shuttle glittered off of Beerlords thighs, gleeming General Lee, off short Andrew Jackson's pillowy stomach, feathers in the sky, streams of source code in the pink glow light.

General Lee held Andrew Jackson as Beerlord helped the extraterrestrials back into the loading bay.

'A Walk From Annunciation Square To Bunny Friend Park'

"Like the author, quill in pinch, writing a narrative, and calling it fate."

"Lawmakers were saying they have been very concerned about this, the President's dangerousness, the dangers that his mental instability poses on the nation," Lee told CNN in a phone interview Thursday.{{21}}

"I remember when we were using rusty old electric guitar strings threaded through the eyes of our harps. Not tuned to anything in particular. Buzz and dissonance, and maybe one happenstance fifth. Plucking and forgetting, all the lead melting into our bodies of fire."

"Drinking mercurial bloody marys."

"Your harp with the patterns of arsenic and beryllium, flooring for the robed and bearded white chalk outlines of lyre player, seated facing the soundhole, and the other lyre player, both bowing in perverse vibration, the base of the lyres connected to the bottom tip of tail and chakra, electric glass shards."

"In the Menstruum!"

"Like in Ken Russell's Song of Summer, carrying the body of the composer."

"I'd rather imagine Delius along the St. John. Sick of orange juice."

"Kathleen Turner in Baby Geniuses?"

"I keep having these dreams that are seemingly narrated by Dom DeLuise."

"He's dead now."

"How can you remember..."

"And then, I feel this dull ache between my ears, like a black hole forming."

"Itchy Itchiford in the scrapyards of New Orleans!"

After his first long-duration flight, which lasted 159 days, Kelly wrote that doctors found swelling of his optic nerve as well as choroidal folds, similar to stretch marks, on his eye.

NASA researchers have identified these and other eye problems, such as the flattening of eye shape, in many male astronauts on long-duration space missions.{{22}}

"Plasmodium Ovale, Plasmodium Malariae, Plasmodium Vivax,

Plasmodium Falciparum."

"And to speak of the molecular pathogenesis!"

"Trichomonas vaginalis!"

"The empty plinth of P.G. Toutant-Beauregard. The ghost of Donald Sutherland in the made for tv movie The Hunley."

"Psychostimulant sounds! Inducing Alpha, Beta, Theta, Delta brainwaves with specific audio frequencies."

"New Orleans after the new years."

"They had two dozen cruise ships lined up. Looking down on the city from the river like prison tower guards. They were mining for relics, big conveyor belts spitting away sand and shell. But most importantly the glass from beer bottles."

"If you think of it. This entire town is a mound of glass from the bottles of spirits."

"The reefer muggles."

"If you get high enough, and say their names slowly, without any intention, its like remembering."

"The Animule Dance."

"Manuel Manetta."

"King Oliver and Louis Armstrong. Johnny Dodds and Baby Dodds."

"Jellyroll. Papa Tio. John Robichaux. Tony Jackson."

"Bunk Johnson's teeth."

"Odysseus and Telemachus."

"Over the lake water at Milneburg."

"Next to the canal water on Perdido."

"Parler! La Musique!"

"Clarence Williams. Alphonse Picou."

"The shine on Rampart street."

"Basin Street!"

"Andrew Jackson wore a punk rock vest with an Amebix back patch walking from Jackson Square down river on Decatur, cuts up Frenchmen towards the lake, makes the rounds, turns right on Saint Claude, everything was burned out, syringes like sand, he had a knife at waist, smells like ghost town and fear, only poisonous caterpillars bloomed."

"And that's why they say they drink."

"Trumpet in the distance."

"The rhythms of the I-10 Claiborne Overpass, cars sputter exhaust, tires tread heavy pop slide."

"Mickey Mouse, Daisy Duck, Donald Duck, Minnie Mouse,

Goofy, Pluto, Dumbo, Ariel, Scrooge McDuck, Launchpad
McQuack, Huey, Dewey, Louie, Snow White, Bambi, Baloo,
Bagheera, Shere Khan, Mowgli, Kaa, Little John, Robin Hood,
Peter Pan, Jiminy Cricket, Gepetto, Pocahontas..."

"Porky Pig versus the anarchist!"

"Ether, Gasoline, GHB!"

"Nitrous, Poppers, Nutmeg."

"Salvia, DMT, Mescaline, Ayahuasca, Ibogaine, White Flour."

"Ketamine, PCP, Marijuana, Domino Sugar."

"Morning Glory and Psilocybe."

"Holy Basil and Methamphetamine and Indigo."

"You ever noticed how Daffy Duck stays the same age, from
back when we was a kid, everything else has changed... you, me,
the world, everything. But Daffy Duck, is the same."

"Goddess, it is hard for a man to recognize you at sight, however
knowledgeable he may be, for you have a way of donning all
kinds of disguises."

"And Bugs Bunny too. And Morgus."

"Nikola Tesla and Madame Blavatsky ate beignets at Cafe Du
Monde, sort of like, a date. Helena poured her cafe au lait over
hers, to make a runny syrup for the dipping. Nikola
meticulously quartered his with a fork and knife into small clean

bites."

"Pascal B. Randolph wrote things about himself he didn't like and burned the paper they were written on, letting the ashes fly in the wind out over the Mississippi river."

"When he was naked after a long disheveled night of drinking, coming to in the bed of someone who's name he couldn't recall, Andrew Jackson would stretch his limbs in the bathroom mirror, admiring the tattoos that covered his muscles. Thinking about graffiti."

"Marie Catherine Laveau was upset that New Orleans was on the internet. Not too long ago things were reversed, and she would scoff at the notion, insisting the permanence of orality."

"That black light painting by George Catlin of the space buffalo of Venus, furry crown and stare."

"Guy Davenport buckled his gravity suit to update it's firmware. The connection to the network was weak. Sputtering fragments. A rabid bat died against his front door."

'The Bad Kids Club and the Mystery of Fiesta Plaza'

Bloated and fleshy plump Andrew Jackson toothlessly sucked down sugar water. The left side of his face was melting. The intergalactic travel times in and out of the New Orleans Metropolis were sickening. The fishy smell of cutting the head off a swamp frog and throwing its wriggling torso plop back in the mud. Andrew Jackson turned his one awful eye.

His space ship had been in traffic. "This damn town. Too many anniversaries."

Andrew loaded an incoming video message on his screen: "Jackson babe, we seemed to have located a series of anomalies. How'd you like the eighties?"

"The SS Columbia's voyage around Cape Horn? Swell chronometrics."

"More like MS Athina B beached upon Brighton. You see, these anomalies are beginning to erase certain well placed perimeters, so we need you to investigate, specifically insure that the

Honorable Judge Babylon is able to make a certain transaction."

At that moment the camera pulls back, Andrew Jackson's clothes are ripped away by invisible netting to reveal a sequined and bedazzled leotard. He is atop a pyramid of fleshy bodies, like kaleidoscopic Busby Berkely waterfall. Gold tinted Vaseline camera lens. A chorus line chant of, "Money, Power."

If you go down Read Boulevard you can find the Fiesta Plaza with the smell of popcorn and fried crisp, and kids laughing and skating on ice while their parents hold plastic bags like totem, off in some hidden speaker array Diana Ross and Lionel Ritchie sing 'Endless Love,' the grand avenues of the Lake Forest Plaza. The glorious Santa Clara with hollowed bannisters and colonnade. The much lauded and admired Santa Ana. The storied and immortal Santa Maria. The eternal thoroughfare Santa Rosa. Such sacred Saints of commerce. Cartoon birds of gold flew in the air carrying a banner that read, "Celebrate! Lake Forest Plaza! Celebrate!" It was a time of youth. The mall was becoming a myth. The sound of children at frolic, a rumbling thunder.

Off, away, down an inconspicuous corridor of the clover leaf architecture, back around and to the side of the D.H. Holmes, around down through the passageway behind the fluorescent light, you would never know except the occasional smudge of chocolate or stray candy, down past the false wall that would swivel, up the winding staircase where there was a convenient escape hatch leading out to a Baskin Robbins, but a little further, and squeeze through that thin sliver to discover the Bad Kids Club. A motley gang of meddling kids intent on solving the mysteries of life. They had even formed a corporation for their secret society succinctly titled, Mysteries. "Incorporation is all the rage these days," Daphne would smile when they were hanging drywall and building secret corridors. Norville with an ever archaic affair for pickled cucumbers, munched off in the corner of their secret club house, soundlessly chanting the mantra, "Bad Kids for Life."

The Bad Kids Club was started soon after the mall was built. Daphne and Velma were involved in uncovering a secret tea smuggling operation. The Yaka-Mein Mafia were soaking holly leaves in carcinogenic sludge from the Mississippi river and marketing it as Pu-erh Tea. Norville was sneaking cheese pizza from the lunch court when he over heard the mafia men say, "We have the fake poo air (Pu-erh) ready for pickup." Norville thought that synthetic farts penetrated the fine line that humanity should not cross in its lust to become manufacturing Gods and quickly informed the girls who after further investigation found that instead of methanous mayhem, the case was one of cancer, corporate abuse, and crazed killers, and that the illicit tea was stored in a secret space between the walls of the mall, revealed at just the right moment with a secret trap door button operated by the food court soda fountain machine, which was activated by the pressing of all flavors at once, sending pu-erh crates to flight, which karmically Norville happened to have caused, succumbing to thirst, whilst evading capture. The Yaka-Mein Mafia was taken down with a cry of, "Meddling Kids." And the Bad Kids Club moved into the vacant space. "Renovation!"

"I heard that since we took those Mafia guys down, theres not much Yaka-mein around town anymore, places still have the sign, but you go inside and ask for a bowl and it's like they never heard of it."

"There'll always be Yaka-mein."

Norville made a list and then read it: "First order of business, we gotta get some snacks man, I'm freaking out."

"Norville your belly must've ate up your brain. I bet you can't even name five presidents of these United States."

"You can't fool me Daphne. I know there's only one president."

The Bad Kids Club would indulge diversions with reckless jouissance. Norville would spend his days in the food court, gleaning to dine. Bouncing about with the grace of an insect carrying a boulder of bread crumb, stacking high plates of food, flinging scraps in flourished arcs from trash bins. Diving into dumpsters like poised for Olympic greatness. "Oooh, a little bit of chocolate syrup, a half eaten donut, still warm too! Some fried chicken, a little chow mein, pork chop with a bite missing, yes please, french fries, mmm sprinkles..."

"I swear he has parasites, how he eats so much."

"Gene Keys, we don't have health insurance so I guess..."

"Oh no Velma, No way. You're not getting me to eat tobacco again. I'm not swallowing any more cigarettes!"

"Norville! You have parasites!"

"Well then... I'll have to eat a little extra for them, won't I."

At night Velma and Daphne would sneak into the lingerie store together and play with each others bodies, laughing while costuming different games of dress-up and touch. Sometimes Norville would be invited, but he was such a sloppy kisser, not patient in the least.

"Shhh... or Norville will hear, boys just don't know how to do it right."

"Would you want to live in a world invented by us kids?"

"Yes...please. Right there, don't...stop..."

"The other day, Norville was chased by this old lady. She kept following him yelling, 'I don't want to be forgotten. Please remember me.' Norville was scared. He didn't even know her."

"I was like, zoynxs lady, you got the wrong guy. She kept saying, 'Please remember. Please remember me.' It freaked me out like jeeze. I just wanted to get past her cause I smelled a freshly dumped cheese and pickle pizza pie calling me from the food court and she grabbed me and held me under her, staring in my eyes with such alarm and terror, zoynxs!"

"Please remember me. I don't want to be forgotten. I'm eighty years old. I've been around here for eighty years, but everything is gone. Nothing is here. Please. Please remember me. Everything is disappearing. Please remember me. I don't want to disappear too. Please remember me. Please remember me."

"I finally got past her at the jewelry shop, slid under Old Man Jenkins hip spaced legs and crawled through the air duct."

"Betcha Old Man Jenkins wasn't too happy about that."

"No way! He said he was gonna get me when I least expected it. Just my luck."

"Who do you think that lady was?"

"What lady?"

"It's a mystery!"

"The lady who didn't want to be forgotten."

Norville gripped his shirt until his hands became waxy, skin like melted candles, shaking, small squirts of urine fell into his underwear.

"Oh man..."

"Norville, what are you doing?"

"Landre, Landreau, Landrey, Landri, Landrie, Landrieu, Landry, Like Zoynxs! Broussard, Blanchard, Blanchet...Moten, Motoun, Moton..., ...I'm reading the phone book to see if I can figure out who that lady was, so many names... She has to be in here. I keep blaming myself for forgetting her. Like zoynxs, I still don't know who the heck she is. She just freaked me out, man."

"Oh Norville! It's ok, it's not your fault. Wait! I've got an idea Norvy, lets go check the tape from the security cameras, maybe they'll provide a clue."

For Christmas this year there was a full size mascot suited Mister Bingle roaming the halls, photo ops by the Maison Blanche, hugging the children of customers, making their plastic bags pregnant with squeeze. Security Guard Bleachy, cultivating a haze of noir, had been watching Mister Bingle, something didn't seem quite right, it was difficult to verbalize the particulars, sort of like an unexpected taste before a seizure. "Yeah, I've been watching Mister Bingle, he keeps going back near this emergency exit by the theaters. At first I thought, ok, maybe the guy likes to take a little nip, you know, hit the sauce, but then I started to watch closer. See, look, wait for it, right there. Did you see it? I'll rewind and play it again, see if I can pause the tape right, there. I think it's that woman you were describing. And look there, it's one other person."

"Thanks for the intelligence Security Guard Bleachy."

"We gotta go find Mister Bingle and ask him some questions. Lets go gang."

"I was hoping you wouldn't say that, zoynxs..."

After the last janitor empties their mop bucket and Olivia Newton John fades, and the doors lock, a different sort of life starts at Lake Forest Plaza, Norville felt best at these moments, like the mice in a scurry-filled pleasure dome off in the shadows, but not tonight, because those same comforting familiar shadows were more sinister. There was a darkness unlike before.

"I don't understand what happened today."

"We said we wouldn't talk about it for a minute."

"But he was...he was cutting off pieces of..."

"Enough, Velma! I can't take it. I need a few minutes."

"Zoynxs!"

"He was cutting off pieces of his own body!"

"I said no! No!"

"Zoynxs! Like..."

"There was nothing there under the mascot suit... what was holding his body together? Was it some sort of projection lens? It had to be an illusion... but the blood. Gene Keys, this is troubling..."

"And zoynxs, he was saying 'Babble On,' like, cutting deep, man, freaking me out..."

"It was like he was doing a routine, like cutting up a mushy potato."

"Yeah, I heard that too Norville, he said, 'Stop Babbling On,' that means to stop talking uncontrollably. To babble is to just talk without meaning, so to stop babbling on, means to stop talking without meaning, what does that mean?"

"Like, I don't know Velma, but I, like, won't babble on any more. I'm done."

"His face didn't even register with what he was doing to himself..."

"Say that again Norville."

"I'm done?"

"No, you said, you won't Babylon anymore."

"Yeah. So."

"Babylon! Not babble on. Judge Babylon! That old guy, the walking wattle and snood, who wears that fancy all white suit and vest to the food court and always orders the barbecue and never, never once has he spoiled his clothing! I knew he must've been mixed up in this."

"Zoynxs! That guy gives me the ca-ca-ca-creeps."

Daphne would lay in the fountain at night, bristling the coins thrown in for luck across her hands, paddling in circles, the smell of chlorine, singing to herself, as if in song, "Am I complicit with these horrors by living off its waste?" Velma would lay on the tile nearby, in her underwear, her hand drifting in the water, eyes swimming along the waves of Daphne's shoulders, her stomach on the cold marble. That night, waking from a dream where she couldn't breathe Velma threw her arms out for Daphne's warm body, in a desperate reaffirmation of life by contact, but Velma was alone, and her lungs heaved with weight. Daphne was up on the roof looking out over the lake, "I feel like I'm in a brief moment in time, that is hanging on to existence by the most strangled thread, as if all this, everything before me will fall out from itself, in the briefest lapse of forgetting...That woman..."

"What's up with this place?"

"What do you mean?"

"It's just such a giant building... do you think hundreds of years from now when archaeologists of the future look at the massive ruins of the Lake Forest Plaza, on down to our secret labyrinth in the walls, and Norville's graffito, do you think those future scientists will interpret this structure as a religious center, or a government capitol. Or some center of importance. It's just so big. The ruins must stand through time forever. Don't you think."

"It certainly is a world unto itself. Heck, one minute in the food court alone is more interesting than all the movies playing at the theater right now, and I know, Norville and I have seen them at least half a dozen times each."

"Zoynxs, thirty seconds in the Video Arcade is enough mythological melting pie to leave you satiated for centuries...oh man, do I have a hankering for some eats."

"So here's the plan, I figure we need to tape record Judge Babylon during his lunch. It seems like he's usually discussing business, and maybe he'll say something about that woman and we can figure out who she is and solve this mystery."

"I don't know, sounds sca-sca-scary."

"Quit knee knocking Norville, we need you to control the microphone. You will hide under the table, Velma and I will be close by monitoring the feed."

"Awww man, why did I know I wouldn't like the sound of this..."

Daphne and Velma sat at the table behind Judge Babylon, running the cable for the microphone under an assortment of

oversized Sears bags stuffed with boxes, which concealed the
tape machine. They shared a pair of headphones, sitting side by
side. Norville had gotten into position by a daring operation
involving sliding into place with a skateboard on his stomach.
"Daphne, I'm going to treasure these memories."

"Why are you talking like that?"

"I just... I just..."

"What is it?"

"We need to focus..."

"What is it, Velms?"

"I just... It won't change anything. I shouldn't tell you."

"Now you have to tell me Velma."

"Shh, quiet down. Don't cause a scene."

"...like zoynxs! Are you two picking up my signal? Norville, like
in position, like over and out."

"Andrew, don't think you can threaten me. I know damn well
what I'm doing. We'll have the paperwork any day now."

"I'm here for insurance Judge, your protection. Think of me as a
big ol' comfy cushion, making sure these transitions go
smoothly."

"I just think you're really neat Daphne, thank you."

"Damn your transitions. The old way was working fine. Why change it."

"Daphne. I'm not who you think I am."

"You don't see it? It's already changed, you're left behind."

"The secret of effortless elegance is easily unlocked by Society Brand's stylish and handsome suit. The perfect addition to the well dressed gentleman's wardrobe. Offering a subtlety of expression and comfort only pure wool provides." {{23}}

"There are infinite ways we can take whatever land we want. Buying land is for sheep. It's as easy as removing the people who live somewhere, or adverse possession, spoils of the word. Or the classic, straw man corporation, file a quit-claim deed, do the transfer cleanse. Or hell, the old joker of imminent domain, that one trumps em all."

"Yes yes, quit claim deed and other frauds, the act of one man, but if you transferred your consciousness to the Corporation, we could institutionalize the particulars of your behavior. It's been happening, append your signature. Quit claim the world."

"Like zoynxs, what about clams? Clams are dead? Not Clams! Better not! What about linguine! I like love linguine, man."

"What was that?"

"They're Here! And Godchaux's has them. The Duckhead plain front pant. Pure cotton comfort in a crisp, twill weave. At 22.50 you'll want khaki, navy and olive!"{{24}}

"I was told there was a time disturbance, I knew they'd show up eventually."

Norville with raised chin and zip-tied arms and legs, sweat a sheen of bravado towards his captors. Judge Babylon and Andrew Jackson had him out in darkness in the middle of the ice rink which they had boarded up as if under construction.

"I'm like not gonna tell you meanies anythings."

"Oh really..."

"Like zoynxs! Our secret club house is through the trap door by the Baskin Robbins! I don't want to die."

"Customers loved it and clerks hated it as one of New Orleans' main department stores joined competitors in disregarding Louisiana's Sunday closing laws. D.H. Holmes opened its New Orleans, Houma and Slidell stores, claiming that competitors' Sunday openings forced the company to follow suit." {{25}}

Athene, daughter of aegis-wearing Zeus and King Zulu, salted the alligator skins, rolling them up tight in brine. She waited for the lightning and Elegba. Velma and Daphne would associate the smell of ozone with small details of incomplete memories contained in a particular time and place that always seemed to be.

On Till Morning

Set: Crocodile with clock in stomach.
A time in the future. Space ships pass overhead but none stop.

Special Instruction: Get two different sized containers. Fill the
smaller of the two with water. Pour water from container 1 to
container 2. Pour water from container 2 to container 1. Repeat
until there is no more water.

The Mermaids are an ensemble of twelve, ornately dressed but
fleshy, orgiastic leisure. They speak in unison as well as
individually.

…

Mermaids: With no direction, yes. There is no there. The
ground would swallow things up then move along, but
sometimes, in the bramble, past the oyster shell middens and
mud pits, the grasses had been pushed aside from all the space
ships taking flight, but now stood again.

Yes, here dear. How lovely the comb of time pulls through the
threads of our skull, the sensual touch of the sun. Yes, here my

lovely crab kiss.

Tell them of the soft brush, or the barnacles on our fins.

Or of the pan pipe child, Sweeper Peter, dangling under Chinaberry Tree's in the back-a-town.

Oh, yes! The stories of Sweeper Peter, his escapades at flight, how high up he used to go. The spry faery adventurer, off in the clouds. Such legends.

But now.

Yes, now.

Ambling low, moaning, ruin, he smells of urine and alcohol, shuffling along the sidewalks with a broom sweeping lost change from the cracks. Sitting under that Chinaberry tree all day, living in the past. The white waxy berries falling between his fingers turning rotten.

No, lets tell another story. One with a happy ending.

Why not a happy beginning?

Or a happy middle? All this talk of the end!

There, look now it's Wendy Darling, lips like the sun, voice like the moon. And she is talking to Louis Armstrong, exhaling clouds of smoke, a necklace made of mirrors.

Louis Armstrong: You see, theres more there, Cleavers. Galium Aparine. See those small hooks like velcro.

Wendy Darling: Wow, so magical. They make me feel so alive.

Louis Armstrong: That's the caffeine babe. And here, a
Magnolia tree, Magnolia Grandiflora, such a wonderful spirit.

Mermaids: Louis Armstrong removes some of the inner bark and
puts it to his lips and bites the piece in half. The other, he gives
to Wendy Darling. They walk onto an iron structured building.

Wendy Darling: It looks like one of the space ships, but it's been
left behind.

Louis Armstrong: This, it's an old school, Phillis Wheatley
Elementary. The old canal ran by here years ago. See the right
angles. The patterns of squares. All the windows. The Triangles.
The geometry. Such magical lines.

Wendy Darling: So futuristic!

Tootles: Have ya'll seen Sweeper Pete? He's been messing around
with this new drug that dissociates your organs from your body.
It's like instead of being one unit, you become a multitude of
consciousness. Liver-conscious, lungs-conscious, heart-
conscious, ear-conscious, eye-conscious, it's too much! Tongue-
conscious, genital-conscious! How can one body contain so
many voices!

Wendy Darling: And this one?

Tootles: Poke Salad!

Louis Armstrong: Phytolacca Americana, see the red stem. Poke
baby.

Mermaids: All the lost children hung from the rafters of the Phillis Wheatley Elementary School. Gathered in the courtyards for ceremonies of light, wore smiles under masks.

And they have such fun. Bouncing around, eternal bundles of energy, children forever, covered in glitter, and animal furs. Gathering on crumbling levees at dawn in clouds of thunder, only to send off balloons with brass instrumentation and vim. Their legs straddling wide the air as if walking in a state of lustful joy. Filling their bodies with oxygen. Only to exhale scream and laugh.

One night in a heated lesson on the geometry of music in the courtyard of Phillis Wheatley, Wendy Darling exclaimed a random number generator to be the ideal composer.

Wendy Darling: It's just look, like here. If you start having too much order, too much symmetry, it doesn't work. You can't draw squares and call it music.

Louis Armstrong: I've been to the Pyramids at Giza. I've been to Poverty Point. I know it takes a few squares to make a brick and a few bricks to build a monument. All the numbers, fibonacci, pi, e, Zeno's paradox of consciousness.

R. Williams Spasm Band: The Diminished Seventh Chord is about as symmetric as can be, or the whole-tone scale.

Wendy Darling: That's a magnificent costume R. Williams Spasm Band, is it gold?

R. Williams Spasm Band: Yes, all the old Marigny pirates, living on Love Street, hoarding booty.

Louis Armstrong: Dominique You used to roll with Captain
Hook and Andrew Jackson. Back in those sepia days. Damn
pirates. Murderers. Saints of Capital.

Tootles: All the vibrating strings! Taxodium Distichum

Velma & Daphne: Capitaine, capitaine, voyage ton flag, Allons
chez un autre voisin!

Mermaids: Demandé la charité pour les autres qui viennent nous
rejoindre,
Les autres qui viennent nous rejoindre,
Ouais, au gombo ce soir!

Louis Armstrong: Before all the space ships left, and my granny's
house was bulldozed. The Chinaberry tree... Such wonderful
feathers you have!

Mermaids: Capitaine, capitaine! We must have music for a
parade! How could it be a parade without music? Without
dance? We can gather in the iron rafters of decaying modernist
architecture or along the river, our fins scooping up diamonds of
water. To live inside myth.

That sound! Do you hear it? Look. There. A Second Line down
the street, headed this way. The bass line bounces with step,
moving feet along, Look, it's Sweeper Peter, carrying his broom
like a baton. Smile full of toothless grin, swollen gums of
laughter. Look everyone at Sweeper Peter. Look up! There! Up!

Cites

1 http://www.businessinsider.com/trump-reportedly-said-haitians-have-aids-nigerians-live-in-huts-in-immigration-outburst-2017-12 On Dec 23 2017

2 https://www.washingtonpost.com/news/checkpoint/wp/2017/12/23/theres-a-war-coming-top-marine-corps-general-tells-u-s-troops/?utm_term=.daa6c92229c8 On Dec 23 3017

3 http://www.foxnews.com/us/2017/12/24/ohio-postal-workers-slayings-stun-friends-family-members.html On Dec 24 2017

4 http://newsinfo.inquirer.net/955125/7-children-among-20-killed-in-la-union-christmas-day-collision On Dec 25 2017

5 http://abcnews.go.com/Politics/trump-proud-led-charge-assault-merry-christmas/story?id=51983751 On Dec 25 2017

6 http://www.cnn.com/2017/12/25/europe/topless-protester-baby-jesus-vatican-trnd/index.html On Dec 26 2017

7 https://www.washingtonpost.com/world/russian-warships-skate-close-to-british-waters-over-christmas-holiday-uk-navy-says/2017/12/26/c46bf9b8-ea35-11e7-891f-e7a3c60a93de_story.html?utm_term=.b2ba188a26ec On Dec 26 2017

8 https://www.washingtonpost.com/news/speaking-of-science/wp/2017/12/26/white-house-to-cut-down-magnolia-tree-planted-by-andrew-jackson/?utm_term=.6a68129f6933 On Dec 27 2017

9 http://www.bbc.com/news/world-asia-42500769 On Dec 28 2017

10 https://www.washingtonpost.com/news/post-nation/wp/2017/12/31/five-colorado-deputies-shot-one-fatally-while-responding-to-domestic-call-authorities-say/?utm_term=.f3ae39e2fe24 On Dec 31 2017

11 http://www.cnn.com/2017/12/31/politics/north-korea-trump-mullen-graham/index.html On Dec 31 2017

12 https://www.nytimes.com/2017/12/31/world/asia/afghanistan-suicide-bomber-funeral.html On Dec 31 2017

13 http://www.nola.com/living/index.ssf/2017/12/new_years_ev

e_second-line_new.html On Dec 31 2017

14 https://www.nbcmiami.com/news/local/Miami-Doctors-to-Remove-10-Pound-Tumor-From-Boys-Face-465998283.html On Dec 23 2017.

15 http://www.bbc.com/news/world-us-canada-42465059 On Dec 23 2017

16 https://www.wsj.com/articles/trump-administration-to-grant-mining-leases-that-will-benefit-landlord-of-presidents-daughter-ivanka-trump-1513989674 On Dec 23 2017

17 http://abcnews.go.com/US/wireStory/officers-shoot-kill-gunman-fired-police-51965188 On Dec 23 2017.

18 http://www.foxnews.com/us/2017/12/23/pennsylvania-family-ordered-to-take-down-jesus-christmas-display-after-neighbor-said-it-was-offensive.html On Dec 23 2017

19 http://www.nydailynews.com/news/national/michigan-man-hit-sandbag-thrown-ohio-overpass-dies-article-1.3717500 On Dec 23 2017.

20 http://money.cnn.com/2017/11/13/technology/future-of-fashion-tech/index.html On Dec 23 2017.

21 http://www.cnn.com/2018/01/04/politics/psychiatrist-congress-meeting-trump/index.html On Jan 4 2018.

22 https://www.expressnews.com/news/local/article/Why-can-t-male-astronauts-see-in-space-NASA-12480564.php On Jan 08 2018

23 A-5 Times Picayune/ The States Item Oct 21 1985

24 A-2 Times Picayune/ The States Item Oct 21 1985

25 A-2 Times Picayune/ The States Item Oct 21 1985

{{i}} http://www.foxnews.com/us/2018/03/10/south-carolina-woman-who-gouged-her-eyes-out-thought-it-was-sacrifice-to-god.html On 03/15/18

{{ii}}http://www.nola.com/crime/index.ssf/2018/03/tugboat_sinks_mississippi_rive.html On 03/15/18